Traquant Dieu

Gregory John Ferris

By the same author

*Dedicated to Mark A. Pracko, my best friend*

# PROLOGUE

Paristown was reborn. It remained to be seen if the years-long attempt to revitalize a slice of France in Louisville would endure. The town had lost close connection to its initial French roots over the intervening centuries that had seen like larger cities to the east, waves of immigration.

Discovered by a Frenchman and once part of New France, the best-known ethnic part of the town had long been Germantown.

Remnants of its Franco past remained: the statue of Louis Seize in front of the courthouse, longstanding student exchange programs between the University of Louisville, Sister Cites, and the southern French town of Montpellier. The local Alliance Française was accessible and doing well, and there was talk of major league soccer coming to town. That would surely require French players.

Paristown was new. Its grand opening had been a few days ago; the day was warm, and the crowd was large and enthusiastic in seeing a section of Louisville's forgotten past being rejuvenated. Time would tell, as it did with all things. There was hope that it would become a tradition, as Forecastle had, and the Derby a century earlier.

Detective Percheron was there in no official capacity. It was a rare day off. He was as familiar as anyone in the city with its roots, with his own French roots, and felt guilty that he had not pursued it, despite his parents' urging. Maybe after retirement, an event approaching at a pace like the gallop of horses at Churchill Downs, the famed track itself a few miles distant.

Retirement, he put the chilling concept as far out his mind as he could. He paused, simply to relish the serenity that lack of motion provided. The day, very warm and sunny, the crowd, calm. It was the sort of peaceful moment that he and his colleagues struggled to maintain.

He was more likely to be in pursuit of the murderer of a current resident than free and idle to study the lives of residents long dead, French immigrants or otherwise.

Percheron started again at a lugubrious pace, but soon paused, this time before a temporary bulletin board that stood next to a permanent schematic of the venue. A young man turned, leaving space for Percheron to step forward to read the various advertisements. There were numerous, colorful sheets promoting various French themed events: meetup groups, film festivals, classes at the Alliance Française, specialized tours, local restaurants.

One flyer caught his attention. Entitled Traquant Dieu, it was printed in both French and English. It advertised a new game coming to Louisville. The flyer mentioned visits to various churches and other religious sights as part of the activities.

That might be interesting, he thought. He rarely had occasion to visit the less seedy parts of town. At least his wardrobe was suitable for all occasions. He alternated between suits and slacks and sportscoats. One of his nieces, not yet great, had followed him into police work. It had been with a mixture of pride and disappointment that he had learned of her decision. Over time his disappointment had faded to nothing.

His niece had recently been promoted to detective, and he relied now on her to select new clothes when necessary. She appreciated the limits to style that their shared occupation demanded, and she saw no hidden meaning in choosing her uncle's dress wear, a task various women friends had performed when he had relied on them.

He noticed a phone number at the bottom of the Traquant Dieu flyer. Text for more information it read. He sighed at the in fashion, inescapable four-letter word: Text. Damn. Nevertheless, the detective reread the entire document, attentive to signs that this might be just another new religion gambit. So far, nothing indicated anything other than a fun, educational diversion.

His instincts kicked in, or perhaps it was just habit, for he glanced quickly around at the crowd.

It was peaceful, nothing was obviously amiss. He would need to get used to the monotone of retirement. He might liven it up with texts, he said in a mental jab at himself.

The game promised both COSPLAY and IRL experiences. Percheron was unable to translate those words into anything more meaningful other that they probably meant he was too old to play.

He moved on. Despite its name, Paristown offered non-French activities and food. He wondered if it was an attempt to create a permanent version of Worldfest held each September on the Belvedere, with French at its center.

It certainly qualified as far as American history. Custer himself, of the eponymous last stand had recruited for his seventh calvary in this part of town.

A world fair of sorts had stood not far to the west, and Edison himself had resided in Louisville.

Cassius Clay, Muhammed Ali, was the best-known native son. His image and that of other now national notables adorned various buildings around the town. God, how thankful he was that he would not have to suffer that fate.

# CHAPTER ONE

Eddy was bored and irritated.

Why had he come here, to this cemetery? Why did he do anything these days?

Boredom. Eddy imagined that he could raise his eyes skyward and see an airplane trailing a banner with the offensive word blazing in large letters, chartered solely for his annoyance. He scowled, refusing to succumb to temptation. Eddy was also hungover, but that too was his fault. He half wished that it was a brain tumor so he would be relieved of responsibility. It was only a half wish, for he could no longer summon a complete desire.

Boredom. He was tired of the word and the sickness that it was, a disease to which he had felt immunity. Until, until when? Long enough ago that he could not pinpoint an exact date. It was an event unworthy of being commemorated. He struggled with it, and yet now, after these many months, boredom had become an enemy so familiar that he was ambivalent as to which of them won. What would constitute victory?

Saturday was bar day, Sunday was church day, and Monday was his weekly visit to the allergist. He had expected that one of them would set him right, or correct the other two, and perhaps it had,

1

for he had finally decided to reserve the seventh day for missing church.

A graveyard was an odd place to begin a new day, let alone a new life. The well written flyer at Paristown had promised excitement. Eddy was old enough to still place value in words inscribed on paper. A person had made the effort that online ads did not require. It was what he would have done. If he had not been bored, that is.

It was supposed to be fun, a challenge to the purveyor of existence itself. A game of sorts.

The game, Traquant Dieu. Visiting houses of worship, viewing hidden passages, deciphering hidden and lost meanings in statues, windows, grave markers. All this within the two-hundred-year history of Louisville. Whether or not contrived clues were to be part of the game, was not disclosed, but what harm could it be to attend a few of the meetings. He noticed that the flyer had a website for more information but indicated that the game was played in person. Thank goodness, he thought.

There should be a victim. Don't all games include a victim, regardless of which term is used? Where was the body? He was sure that he had left a body somewhere on the grounds. Above ground, he chuckled to himself. Otherwise, any such game set in a graveyard would be over.

Eddy turned around slowly, studying the homes that nearly surrounded one of Louisville's oldest cemeteries. Nondescript dwellings lay beyond the chain link fence that separated the dead from their successors. The barrier was entwined with weeds and shrubs, some vibrant, others desiccated.

It was a pitiful frontier between those who mattered only a little, and those who mattered not at all.

Eddy recalled a friend of his who had looked down on everyone as either snobs or scum. For him there had been no ideal position in society for anyone to occupy, leaving the entire human race open to mockery, he and Eddy included. The friend had moved away, leaving Eddy without a conscience. Whether that had been a curse or a gift, Eddy had still not decided. He was still bored. And irritated. Above all, he was late.

He saw no one about on either side of the barrier, for it was early morning. The cemetery itself was relatively clean, most of the windblown debris captured by the semi vigilant chain link guard. At the far end of the graveyard a tarp lay, one corner flapping in the slight breeze.

Eddy was late. He was supposed to have been here an hour ago.

His phone alarm had lacked the power to overcome the amount of alcohol he had consumed. It had been even less effective since he had failed to set it.

He regarded the nearby houses. There was not a person to be seen. The same solitude enveloped the few hundred stone markers. None of the graves were recently turned. None of the neighboring dwellings were freshly painted. All inhabitants were as equally invisible and lethargic this warm Sunday morning.

Ennui. The word came to him as he studied one of tombstones, the fading words to mark the final resting place of a French immigrant. Perhaps this long-dead stranger had the answer to the only important question, but his capacity to speak to Eddy in any language had long since withered away.

The community remained mute, uncooperative. Eddy moved to kick one of the recalcitrant rocks but refrained from doing so. His inaction was not due to respect. Eddy intended to run later, and a sore or swollen toe would prevent it.

Should he ask the neighbors? Was one of them watching him surreptitiously from behind a curtain, laughing at Eddy's gullibility? Should he knock on a few doors? That might result in his being shot. At best, he would receive no information.

Despite being a quiet neighborhood, distant enough from the freeway, one could almost hear the persistent hum of decay working overtime. The rot ignored the growing frequency of curfews and laughed at the sound of daytime gunshots.

Those shot and killed in this ward would be interred elsewhere, for this territory was full and spoken for. The newly dead would be likely missed by their families, for a while, but not by God. No, those dead, and those unseen behind the visible walls, were unimportant, semi-safe like the residents in the game he had hoped to learn more about this morning.

The cemetery was vacant of any potential players. He had had to use Apple maps to arrive here himself, for some reason Google had problems providing correct directions in the slice of town between I-65 and the river.

His invitation had come in response to the text message he had sent to the number on the Paristown flyer. He had sent the text after one or two too many drinks.

He regarded the tombstones; he and they had time today. One marker bore the same last name as his; a distant relative, he wondered. It did not matter, what would they have in common if the woman long dead rose from ground this moment and said good morning. Or would it be bonjour, or guten tag? What would they say to one another?

Still, the coincidence bothered him, for theirs was not a common name.

No one was going to show. He crumpled the flyer in his hand and tossed it on the ground. The soft sigh as the ball of paper touched grass was as satisfying to Eddy as if he had kicked one of the worn markers of human existence.

Ghosted in a cemetery, he thought bitterly.

He would create his own game. It would be what this one could not be, more than a sheet of balled paper sitting abandoned in a graveyard, surprisingly clean for being nearly full. Aside from a tarp covering what was likely the dirt destined to cover a rare, new arrival, there was no debris. Nothing to keep the flyer company. A slight breeze picked up and the paper began to roll after the departing human. The wind ceased abruptly, and the advertisement came to a stop next to the tarp covered mound.

The game would be his, Eddy cheered himself with the sudden thought. An entire universe at his command.

The neighborhood was still devoid of human sightings as Eddy started the engine of his car. In the rearview mirror he noticed a single homeless woman pushing the ubiquitous shopping cart, the sole possession of domestic refugees, and even that was borrowed. In a country where even the dead had permanent residences, only she and her tribe remained unregistered. He continued to watch as she and her mobile estate entered the graveyard, the wheels of the metal cart respectfully silent. Not a single squeal pierced the silence of the woman's move into her new neighborhood, praying that here at last the residents would not demand her eviction.

Eddy drove rapidly East on I-64, the Ohio river on his left pouring itself slowly westerly. To his right, he observed the steeples of several traditional churches. It was clear this morning, the sky blue and cloudless, the river less brown, its water no longer cluttered with tree trunks and other debris from storms the previous week.

Eddy was disappointed, for he had relished the temptation that the flyer had dangled before him. Its allure had supplanted boredom.

People were such flakes, Eddy thought. But gamers were supposed to be different. They believed in something, if only in the rules that surrounded that something.

Believers of all sorts were unforgiving sticklers for rules. The upside was that the rules had changed. Games came and went, as did cults and new religions. Each game had its canon and user guide. They rose and fell out and favor and were disposed of sooner or later. Hell, the numerous rules books had been sent to landfills across the nation.

Deities and Demons, was that a game, or a religion? He had imagined and abandoned so many ideas, a few in the same minute. He would need to do a quick internet search to see if anyone had copyrighted the name. Somewhere in the back of his mind, still a bit blurred from the alcohol of the night before, the game seemed familiar. He must be conflating the flyer and his lack of memory from the previous evening. The booze was getting out of control. Worse, it was taking control.

Good and evil, that was the essence of play. Man had supplanted both good and evil. There remained little space for deity or demon. To all evidence, they had come to terms with their redundancy. The fact was obvious in their continued absence.

He thought of the articles of faith, user guides for newbies, composting like the faithful, in burial grounds where nothing resprouted from the soil. In his games, respawning was common, expected, nonmiraculous. He was good at games.

All those printed and carved admonishments, the good punishing the bad.

Eddy thought of his software teams and their performance. It came down to design versus execution. A great idea, poorly executed, was destined to be a fantastic flop.

Like Traquant Dieu. No, that was wrong. It had an intriguing but weak design accompanied by no execution. It had failed on the first hurdle, and it lay crumpled in the uncared-for cemetery that became more distant each passing second.

He would have done much better. He would do much better, he said aloud. Eddy thought better when moving. Walking, or running, or driving, ideas came through motion.

It could have been his creation. Who was to say it wasn't? Some anonymous poster and sender of one email? It could have been an errant bot, one of his own forgotten creations. No one showed in real life. The game was a bust, a lame first effort.

Still, there had been a kernel of value in the idea, he would scoop up the abandoned nugget of gold and refine it into a spectacular coin, adorned with his own image.

Good harassing evil until the gods themselves grew tired of its monstrosity. The story had been recounted ad nauseum. It was boring and ready to be buried. Besides, it did not work. God no longer cared, while the devil, if he had not committed suicide, was enjoying an ill-deserved retirement.

The real game called for disruption. Disruption was Eddy's forte. He considered a name change. Traquant Dieu? Really? Perhaps Deities and Demons? That sounded worse he decided. A name change would constitute more form versus function. He would focus on function. The flyers had already been printed. The name would remain. That was all that would survive his makeover.

Why search a mystical cup when one could stalk God. "Traquant Dieu," he said,

Good over evil would become instead evil over good. Wasn't that the purpose of man? Evil over good? It was time for a great upset. The hour had come for God to play Eddy's game. Traquant Dieu indeed. And if the devil wanted to play, he would just have to come out of retirement.

He critiqued the game in his mind, improved it, and adopted it as his own before he reached the second loop that encircled his town. Eddy felt a little less bored. God, it felt great. Almost.

# CHAPTER TWO

Stalking God was proving to be a chore.

If there was a game master, he was as absent at home as he'd been at the cemetery. Eddy had gone to multiple places where the supreme being was said to be, but the boss appeared to be seriously resting. He had gone alone into His homes, and for someone who created billions of humans, He seemed inordinately shy. No texts had arrived from either creator.

Eddy had gone to the houses on various weekdays when God should be less busy. No luck.

So many places where He wasn't. Like this one, not quite a palace, but nice enough. It was as if Louisville's Central Park in town was reserved solely for a handful of plays, where the script was confusing despite modern translation, and where the cast for the annual Shakespeare in the park performances were no shows.

This building and its counterparts -- vacant. Pretty, some ostentatious, all serious, but empty, nothing but an exquisite shell, void of the content one was expected to adore.

A few words of scripture were visible here and there. Nothing modern. Why had they stopped recording their history? They had effective writers back in those days. Why did they ever stop? The bible would outweigh the tax code if they had persevered. It would include an exception for every sin, a punishment for every virtue. A guaranteed best seller.

Shakespeare would have had nothing left to say.

Eddy was secular, profane someone had described him. It was not a sin. He had no exposure to fairy tales of any sort. Only facts and science. It's hard enough to learn anything of value. Why clutter your mind with ravings and fantasy. Which made him an excellent gamer and game maker.

He was made for an electronic world that was endless.

Sports, fantasized life in its own right, was bland compared to their electron energized fantasia augmented versions. The Super Bowl could be set in 1939 Kansas, smack in the city of Oz.

Real sport was an oxymoron, having lost is righteous violence. It had devolved to an occasion for similarly gendered athletes to embrace one another in false and forced displays of emotion.

Games are meant to be left behind at some point and Eddy was on the verge of regretting that he had started this one. He had never liked solitaire. When Eddy had stepped into this latest church, he had expected it to be empty. Of other people.

Surely a deity with a history of one-on-one meetings would not demand a large audience today. Man had stopped writing and God had stopped reading.

Eddy was surprised to find a few people were already in attendance, had they all the same idea? If so, they had dressed more respectfully than he had.

No, they were here for another purpose and their numbers increased until the house of worship was nearly full. He considered leaving but his boredom restrained him.

Soon, it was obvious that a funeral service was about to commence. Not long afterward it was evident from the huge attendance and eulogies that the deceased had been a good man.

In the words of one speaker, the deceased was not rich in the way most men described wealth, but exceedingly rich in the way man should define it. But it was another speaker, a nephew, whose story Eddy found the most interesting.

The man began, describing a few moments in the life of himself and his deceased uncle Alfred, who had been apparently a farmer.

"Can anything appear to be of less interest than mud holes?

Yet among the many memories of times past at the farm, there remains to me one in which common mud holes played a prominent role.

In the latter 1980s, the exact year escapes me, I, along with my mother Gertrude and my sister, Sue, were spending several weeks at the farm.

Late one morning, Alfred hitched the iron-wheeled, wooden cart to the larger of his two tractors, the Farmall. He and I drove the short distance to the first gate which lay at the top of a slight ridge. We passed through, continued at a northeasterly direction, and soon reached the tree line.

The road to the first gate was, at that time, dirt. An uneven path, this road was pitted with depressions large and small, each of which would transform into mud holes after a rain. A traversal of this track was at once both bumpy and sloshy.

Interestingly enough, these small ponds did not contain any of the schools of tadpoles which were found in great number in similarly sized pools that one found further back in the woods. Perhaps a biologist more familiar with the fauna of the region could explain why this was so. I suspect that excessive direct sunlight would make for a poor nursery, but I digress.

I mention the absence of tadpoles only to assure the sensitive among us today that no life was taken during this expedition.

At the tree line, Alfred and I descended from the tractor. Following both his instructions and example, I began to gather platter sized flat rocks and to place them in the cart.

I had no idea why we were doing this, but, totally confident in my uncle, I remained silent and proceeded at a healthy clip, gathering and loading.

Alfred must have anticipated my unasked question, as he soon informed me that we were going to fill in some of these perennial mud pits.

Now, to a boy of 11 or 12, filling in mud holes was just as agreeable as walking through them, so I continued at my youthful pace.

In hindsight, the rocks that we gathered were not the best choice, as, consisting mainly of shale, they were themselves, in effect, long dried, compressed mud. They would serve only for a matter of months to repair the road divots. But to be fair, they were what was freely and readily available.

The load nearly complete, I was disconcerted to look up and see that we were surrounded by cows.

A dozen or so of Alfred's bovines had trooped over from the pond in the back pasture, from the area that older relatives referred to as the shingle mill.

At this pond, the cows had been enjoying their own version of a mud hole.

Surrounding us, they simply regarded Alfred and myself. Whether they had come due to boredom, from curiosity, are cows curious, or expecting food, I am not sure, even today. Had they been attracted by the dull sounds of rocks colliding with wood? Who knows.

Me, I like to think that the cows saw themselves as co-managers of the farm. While they normally confined their duties to trimming and fertilizing the pastures, in this instance they seemed to project a keen interest in the general state of the family estate, road conditions included. It's obvious that Alfred raised and retained superior cattle.

The loading was soon complete, and we retraced our steps, stopping periodically to place carefully the rocks in the soon to be former mud holes.

Of course, being only 11 or so, I did toss a few of them from afar, the flat rocks making cannonball splashes as they landed in the water.

Neither Alfred nor the cattle objected.

Sometimes I wish, as we all do, that moments like that lasted forever."

The eulogy over, the speaker sat down. Eddy frowned, annoyed at the syrupy words.

"You're inhuman if you won't stoop to criticizing your fellow men," he wanted to shout.

"No one is that good," he thought.

Eddy pondered, unable to dredge up a comparable memory from his own life. A good part of life is being made privy to family secrets, better yet is to participate in activities that give rise to fresh ones. Eddy's memories were vacant. The only item that came to mind was Le Moo, the restaurant on Lexington Road, and his last date there, last as in final and not the most recent.

Final like this eulogy. Ashes to ashes, dust to mud.

The speeches complete, the tears shed and dried, the attendees left as they arrived, in groups of varying sizes, and in spurts, with the final mourner, nodding at Eddy before passing by as Eddy merely nodded in return but remained silent.

The church left to himself, Eddy wondered if God had left with or as a mourner, or had He missed both appointments set for the day.

Glancing at his watch, Eddy stood, walked the few steps to the entry doors, and left.

# CHAPTER THREE

"On Wheel of Fortune you pay by the letter," the woman, who could have been 40 or near 70, said to detectives Percheron and Zorn. They were standing in Portland Cemetery.

Some cemeteries border on pleasant surroundings. These oases are calm, manicured, green open areas interspersed with sturdy trees resembling well-designed and maintained grounds for the truly retired. This was not one of those graveyards, not after decades of neglect. A chain link fence stood guard along the perimeter, separating the unhappy dead from those alive but no more satisfied than their neighbors.

Portland Cemetery was a burial ground begun in what had once been New France. A few born in old France, come of age in New France, been absorbed into the British Empire, and died as new Americans. The oldest legible marker lay to the west, the marker's inscription 'Des professeurs de foi'.

"Des espères, des prières," detective Percheron said to himself. "All for nought," he continued, gazing at the desolate space.

The faded words on most of the markers were difficult to read. The sentiments inscribed, impossible to comprehend.

Photographs perpetuate the illusion that you can freeze time. Like gravestones, they too deny what lays beneath.

The woman of indeterminate age stood silent, expectant. Her own wheel had been on the downward swing for a while and was visibly stuck at its nadir, the policemen observed. Misfortune would be her permanent residence for whatever time remained to her.

"I remember three letters of the plate, that will be sixty dollars," she said confidently.

"No three for fifty?" countered the younger detective.

The look of powerlessness on the woman's face that his ill-timed humor elicited brought instant regret to the detective.

"Sixty dollars," he agreed in embarrassed retreat.

Annie stretched out a hand. A slight trembling was noticeable. It was not the vibration of life but a tremor of illness.

Or maybe it was constant fear, Percheron considered.

The flood plain on the left bank of the Ohio, below the falls was very near, an unofficial park for the reckless.

It was the first developed area of Louisville, but which now was the least developed. It separated downtown from the impoverished region to the west, a combination of wild new world and the savagery of nature. It was a damp refugee for the homeless. To most people, these fellow humans were as invisible as the ghosts that they desperately seek.

"Pay me," Annie commanded with feigned confidence. "Sonny, it's just like Wheel of Fortune or witness protection." She laughed among the dead.

She waited until three bills were in hand before she stated,

"187. Those were the first three letters."

"Those are numbers."

"Whatever."

"And the other letters?" Percheron asked.

"That would be a guess," she replied as she slipped her wages into one of the many pockets her grimy outfit sported. Her honesty gave the detectives pause.

"Kentucky plates?"

"Yeah, regular."

In response to their puzzled expressions, she added,

"You know, not a vanity plate. I had one of those in another world."

Percheron chose not to pursue the invitation to her life.

"And the vehicle itself? Was it a car, an SUV? What color was it?"

"A car, either blue or grey. Or maybe green."

A moment later she added, "It was a bright morning. You know how it is."

"The driver?" Zorn asked.

"What color do you want him to be? Or do you prefer a woman? We all have quotas."

"Ours is for the truth," Zorn replied.

"Truth never makes its quota."

For a moment, Percheron wondered if the woman was reciting everlasting words from the surrounding stones but decided that she was naturally witty. Poor, unkempt, smelly when the breeze shifted, but intelligent.

"The truth is what I need," he replied, fighting a desire to see if his words had themselves been stoned.

"The truth is extra."

"Why?" he asked, curious.

"Truth is more precious than gold. Not for me of course. Except maybe today."

"A white male, about 30."

The younger detective glanced at his partner. The same thought had come to them both. Was she describing the actual vehicle, or one from her own real or imagined past? Her statement was not zero, but was it worth sixty dollars? While this woman was the nearest thing to an actual witness, tomorrow she might be dead from a sixty-dollar overdose or drowned in the nearby river either through negligence or design. She could be a victim of a one-woman Thunder over Louisville.

Her death or disappearance would burden rather than aid his investigation, Percheron knew. Not his, but their investigation he reminded himself, sensing the young man beside him. Like the unfortunate woman before him, his partner's presence was an omen that his own last day was approaching. Like life, omens too were fleeting. He could almost feel the second hand of the analogue Timex carve an invisible groove on his forearm, as it raced round and round.

Percheron pondered what he did not know.

19

How did man under tarp die?

How was the body, alive or dead, brought to the cemetery?

In a hearse?

A shopping cart would be hearse enough. They aren't a rare sight, less rare than a hearse would be as this graveyard was full, or nearly so.

Did anyone even keep records, any longer? Percheron seemed to recall that one of his own distant relatives was interred here.

To dump a body in the middle of town, it was a gutsy move. Or did he walk here, drive here?


The woman wandered off after the police had finished their questioning, telling them that if they needed her, she would be around.

I hope so, Percheron thought.

"Any ideas?" Percheron asked his partner.

"When in doubt, its gangs or drugs related?" Ash quipped.

"What about you? Any suspects?"

"Too many, but for now, none of them are promising."

"Or confessing. It's like online dating."

"Oh? Do they trying to murder you there as well?"

"As good as. You haven't tried it, Perch?"

Percheron shook his head briefly.

He understood criminals better than he did the younger generation.

"You are not even certain that the person's sex is as described, let alone if the face, weight, age, or marital status are accurate."

"And it repeats ad nauseum?"

"Yes, nauseating at times."

"I'm not missing anything then. Let's hope we have better success with this cast of possibles. At this point it could include anyone."

"The victim was not bludgeoned here, or was he?"

"I think that he was. But..."

"Perhaps the murderer pretended to be a homeless person?"

"Or a genuine homeless?"

They regarded each other, considering the ramifications of such an outcome.

"I'm not sure which would be worse."

"Did they meet here?"

"For what? It's an odd setting for a meeting."

"An assignation."

"That is quite a word."

"For sex or drugs."

"You are the expert on online dating,"

"I didn't..."

"Would you choose to meet in a cemetery?"

It was the younger man who shook his head in response.

"There is no indication of that. He doesn't come across as the type."

"We are all multiple types, depending on the day. We don't know much about our victim. There is no wallet, no car keys."

"It sounds like robbery, a conk on the head and then off with the wallet and car. He was in the wrong place at the wrong time."

"Why was he in the cemetery, if he arrived there alive? I'll go first. To help someone? Don't be ridiculous," he said a bit loudly, rebuking himself.

"Why not?" the young detective asked, playing devil's advocate.

"Good. Yes. Why not?"

"It is a safe place in a strange way."

"Was there any sign of a homeless camp?"

"Yes. Well not a camp, but one or two people."

"One or two?"

"One."

"And you just paid her sixty dollars."

Percheron considered the possibilities.

Was sixty dollars enough to solve a murder? A bargain at thrice the price. It was week of food for homeless woman. Or a few days of a mealless ride on whatever chemical was on sale. Would the murder be solved by a suicide? It would not be the first time he had acted as lawman and accomplice. He would let another power balance the blood on his hands versus that spilled by others. It was an unsolvable equation, and he chose to ignore it.

While his partner mentally theorized, Ash Zorn reflected on the woman. Ash was one of fraternal twins, born to a woman who herself could have been a near twin to homeless Annie. His mother was perhaps fortunate in having died at an earlier age. His mother had christened him Ashley and his sister Michael. It was unclear if she had named them thus out of spite of their father, intoxication, or as a joke. Later, he and Michael and

discussed and rejected a name swap, as the confusion
was all that remained of their parents

# CHAPTER FOUR

Humor filled the universe. He had read once that a good joke explained existence as well as any three chalkboard equations. He had learned only one equation: Fools equal profits. It was a linear relationship. He had made a fortune, while his face remained unknown, marketing games, fantasies, and error-ridden imaginary to those with too much free time, or not enough time in some cases, he suspected. Nevertheless, the fools' card charges cleared. This new game, your game, he stressed, was better. It was a true game, one he could play for free. Gratis. He liked that word. Maybe that would be his next creation. Gratis, by subscription only. But that would have to wait.

Eddy was online, reading the local news from the previous few days, for news was as sour as new wine if consumed too soon.

The body of a middle-aged man had been found in Portland cemetery, under a tarp. The body had been undisturbed for several days; apparently tarps were not an uncommon sight in graveyards. Eddy thought of the neighborhood and speculated that many occurrences were ignored by the residents.

The man's name was vaguely familiar, Silas Llewellyn. Perhaps their paths had crossed at one time or another. The funeral would be in a few days; Eddy would have to read the man's obituary. Maybe he would attend the service. It would be something to do.

Sure, he was at most an acquaintance, but, but no. The tightening knot in his stomach combined with an elevating heart rate to counsel staying away. He would go to the man's church later, alone. To pay respects. Or not.

Portland cemetery, under a tarp. His memory used to be so sharp. He needed to watch his alcohol consumption.

Eddy tried to recall where he had been the previous few nights, in particular the evening when the body had most likely been hidden in the graveyard. That had to have been at night, didn't it? Did they lock cemetery gates? It was Portland.

The night in question was blacked out in his memory, as he supposed he himself had been.

Had he done something?

He searched for the obituary, at least he would discover which house of worship to visit, to confess or to taunt.

# CHAPTER FIVE

Years ago, Eddy had concluded that his uncle was either trying for the world's record in eccentricity or had taken it upon himself to annoy his nephew into an early grave and inherit his fortune. Still, he was family.

Eddy's uncle sat in the backseat watching a road trip movie on his laptop. It made him feel important to ride in rear, even on the ten-minute ride to the restaurant.

"The country is large enough for separate opinions, but your car is not," he had said to Eddy on their own first so called "road trip".

Eddy pulled into a parking spot, as his uncle closed his laptop.

"This is too far to walk."

'Find another one' was unspoken.

Eddy said nothing but reversed and pulled into one marked handicapped. He had deliberately bypassed the reserved spot, as it was a reminder his passenger typically found annoying.

He put the car in park and was about to stop the engine when his uncle announced a reserved spot even nearer the front door. Eddy obliged and relocated the car one spot over. In total, they had reduced the distance that his companion had to cover by about thirty feet.

Before he turned off the ignition, Eddy turned to face his uncle.

"Is this spot fine?"

"Sure. Why wouldn't it be?"

"It's not too far?"

"I'll manage."

The older man satisfied, Eddy stopped the engine, exited the vehicle, and walked around to the other side, retrieving the walker from the passenger side front seat.

As Robert rolled from the seat, grasping the handles of the aid, he snarled,

"If someone screws with me in my walker, I'll put their ass in a wheelchair, or worse. I can probably walk free one killing."

Eddy looked at his uncle and wondered,

"Will this be me one day?"

On the way to the front door of the restaurant, the word free came to Eddy's mind. Free, walk free, free will, free kill.

Robert was bragging about his walker, telling Eddy for the not first time that the walker was a ninja model, especially designed for the American market, and contained a hidden spot for Caspian pepper spray, or a gun, or both, depending on the size of the defensive weapon the owner selected.

A woman exiting the restaurant stopped to hold the door open for them. Robert stopped his sales pitch and instead thanked the stranger, embarrassed at the role reversal. He really didn't feel that helpless.

"It's only temporary," he muttered over his shoulder as they crossed the threshold.

His mood brightened when he spied one of the waitresses.

"Good, we have Lizzie today," Robert said nodding across the large dining area to a woman in her twenties with perfect posture.

"It is a real shame that she is quitting."

"Oh?" Eddy supplied.

"Yeah, she is moving to Eastern Switzerland with her German boyfriend who she had shared a house with in Albania, after having met him in Turkey. I wish her well, or at least survival."

"Oh?" repeated Eddy.

"Yeah, I've made a note to see if her face appears on 48 Hours someday. I warned her that you can never drop your guard, but what the hell do I know? Old cripples are stupid. Everyone knows that."

After they were seated and had their drinks order taken by the soon to be ex-waitress, Eddy commented on the unknown Lizzie.

"It's a free country."

"Yeah, maybe, but its not a free world.

Not everyone is good you know."

Eddy was content to let his uncle do the talking.

"People have the illusion of self-determination. They make their own future. Then they run into someone who thinks a helluva lot differently."

"Uh-huh."

"Do what you want. Free will some call it. Is it free if you're punished for exercising it? It would be free if it were without consequence."

"Perhaps it is."

"You won't know the correct response until after you've completed the test and returned your answer sheet."

"What?"

"Until you are dead and buried, like that guy they found in Portland cemetery."

Eddy looked at his menu and said nonchalantly,

"Maybe I can cheat?"

"How?"

Eddy shrugged but had already thought of a possible way.

"Points for creativity," he said to his uncle.

He would simply use someone else to take the test for him, Eddy said to himself.

His uncle was rambling on about something else, for he knew the menu by heart.

"You're less than a pawn. Hell, the temperature raises a few degrees and folks lose their minds."

"They are right to worry," Eddy said to keep his uncle on this new topic, whatever it was.

"That is not what I am talking about. The temperature changes them. They are little more than plants, responding to a new heat lamp. Turn off the air conditioning in here, and within an hour all the customers would flee. Likely sue as well. It doesn't help that the judges are nuts too."

"I'll have the usual, Lizzie," he said to the waitress, "the same for my nephew," Robert added, removing free will from one small table in a restaurant in Louisville, Kentucky.

Eddy's uncle sat across from him, watching the cream become one with the coffee. His habit was to pour the sweet white liquid in the hot, caffeinated solution, and let the two reach their own statis. He stared into the swirling mists as if they functioned as a crystal ball. It was his daily consultation at a fraction of a dollar, secure from the designs of perfumed divas who frequented the church that he attended less and less.

"It's cloudy."

"I see that," Eddy agreed, his gaze directed at the warm beverage that stood between them.

"Not this, Eddy," his uncle corrected, his eyes staring in Eddy's, before they both lowered their gaze to the steaming cup.

"It's a witch's brew," Eddy continued, not willing to discuss the weather. Weather was rarely important, and then only as another annoyance.

"It's coffee. They will pass. They will drop no rain, even if we need some, and we don't, but the clouds are nice."

"Nice?"

"Clouds are always nice. They are clear in their intentions; they do their work, and they depart. At my age, they are more and more welcome."

The remark puzzled Eddy, but he said nothing. "We overlook silly talk in children and crazy talk in adults," he thought. Why criticize it in the elderly, when they've had decades to perfect it.

"Don't you get tired of coming here?"

The uncle of Eddy frowned briefly at the question, no doubt annoyed at his nephew's crazy talk, and Eddy blushed. The older man lowered his gaze again, noticed that the coffee had stopped its rotation. It was completely mixed. It was ready. He raised it to his lips and took the tiniest of sips.

"Their movements are like a non-musical carousel. They are a gift, Eddy."

Eddy was hesitant to speak, to continue this conversation that only served as evidence of their mutual delusions, if not madness. If a person recognized their madness did that prove their sanity? If madness could not be recognized by its sufferer, did that gift it as incurable?

"Thank God we live in a region with clouds. Montana, Wyoming, phew. No clouds."

"Really?"

"No happy clouds. Those states see only torn remnants. They are probably used to it. I wonder how they cope?"

"Clouds?" Eddy prompted, his voice flat. "God, this was boring," he thought. "Clouds? Had it come to this?"

An idea came to him, and Eddy regarded his uncle with fresh eyes, and saw for the first time, if not himself, a possible future self. Ghosts of Christmas cloudy.

"Clouds, yes," the uncle replied, terminating Eddy's melancholic train of thought.

"How can one live in a sky filled only with the blue of day and the stars of darkness? Clouds keep me up to date, they remind me that every day is different, each moment unique."

"As you sit in the same café each marvelously unique morning?"

The older man chuckled.

"What is so funny?"

"Each day is different, especially if it is all the same day.  Clouds are one of a kind, like"

"Like us?"

Eddy's uncle nodded.

"Or so I believed."

"You are not sure of your belief?"

"Where is the logic in being sure of a belief? I'm reasonably confident.  That is the joy offered by the clouds.  They confirm that there are no do overs in life, only do somethings.  Isn't that thrilling?"

"Confusing describes you better."

"Life is a roller coaster, a perfect ride, because one of the drops or twists will absolutely kill you. Death with you in the same car, you look up and see the clouds, and you know that this second is real, not a repeat of the one before, that the ride continues. Clouds, Eddy.  Nimbus, Stratus, Cumulus.  Musically angelic names.  What's not to like?"

"I'm working on something new," Eddy offered.

"Where do you come up with this?  As God is my witness, sometimes I believe that you are crazier than me and great uncle Arville combined. That man broke every commandment, or so he said, except murder and suicide."

He laughed at the memory.

"He was quite the character.  As to you, I stop and tell myself that a million people buy your computer games."

"Twelve million. In the US."

"Christ, this planet is screwed."

"I'm going to start dating again," Eddy said in an impromptu confession to the worst possible confessor.

"Christ, is she screwed."

"Was everyone in his family insane?" Eddy asked himself, not for the first time.

# CHAPTER SIX

Detective Percheron noticed the man in St. Matthew's Starbucks immediately. Coming on the heels of his recent encounter with Annie, he was not surprised to spot another homeless person. If that was what the man was. He had learned that a crew had come to town to film a movie set in Los Angeles, with scenes set among a homeless camp. Maybe the Hunger Games had benefited Louisville after all. If being the ideal location of a homeless camp was benefit. Who was he to judge? People still mentioned his hometown when the movie Stripes was discussed.

The man in Starbucks was homeless. At least at first glance. He was unshaven, unstockinged, unbelted, his pants held up by a strip of red cloth that was fastened pirate style. He reminded Percheron of the actor Richard Harris. This man's hair was blondish and longish, tied in a short ponytail. He could have been a hard forty or a not so gnarled 70-year-old.

Yet his hair was clean, as were his shoes. Upon closer examination he was an actor's image of a homeless man. His teeth appeared to be all present, and his movements, while furtive, were a touch overly so, and lacked the jerkiness of addicts.

Whether it was a role or the bitterest of ironies, he was immersed.

On leaving the café, Percheron passed the man and said, "Enjoy your stay."

"Thank you," the man replied courteously.

"Homeless," Percheron said aloud as he settled in his car and sipped his coffee. The victim had been identified, and his car found undisturbed. Percheron had spoken to one armed tow truck driver at the scene near Six Mile Lane, far from Portland Cemetery. It had been fascinating to watch the tow operator perform the complicated steps to load the vehicle, relying on the aid of a well-used broom handle for the more cumbersome tasks. Despite his efforts, and those of the forensics team, the car had provided no clues.

Instead, as he sat in his own car, Percheron replayed the conversation with the widow of the victim in his mind. They had identified the man as Silas Llewellyn, a town native who, while not a public figure, was broadly involved in community affairs, from Sister Cities to Worldfest, any activity that served to bring various ethnic groups together under one group, or in the case of Worldfest, on the Belvedere next to the Ohio river. He also worked a great deal with the homeless. It was not surprising then that he had been found where he had.

"He would meet anyone, anywhere, if they needed help, or wanted to offer help. You'd be surprised at how shy some affluent people can be."

Percheron had nodded in the affirmative.

"He was like one of yours," she had continued, "or how I imagine one of your undercover cops might work. Quiet, unassuming, until the big bust. Except in Silas' case not a bust, but a break for someone. A job, a scholarship, yes, a party, but it was not really about a party, not for anyone who was involved, not for Silas."

She had said more, but those few sentences had given him a sense of the man.

"Homeless," the detective repeated. He would need to speak to Annie again.

It would be a pity if Silas Llewellyn had been killed by someone he had been intent on helping.

# CHAPTER SEVEN

"Do you think his wife killed him?" Ash asked Percheron one morning, a few days later.

"The doctor?" Percheron asked unnecessarily in return, for the local news was full of nothing else. A man found dead in the west end, why, that was hard to compete with suspicious death in a family of well-known Jewish doctors. The public had already decided that the Portland killing had tawdry roots, while this new death was juicy enough for a genuine Hollywood movie. Perhaps the Richard Harris lookalike would audition for a role, Percheron thought.

"Yeah. A real medical doctor. Poisoned, they say. The wife would know about poisons."

"As would any sixth grader with an internet connection. Translated into any language, free of charge."

Ash took hold of the conversation, providing the dialogue for both he and Percheron.

"The wife reported the death from their house. After returning home from a picnic."

"A bluff?"

"A bluff of what? She can't not report that her husband is dead."

"He was poisoned at the picnic, with hundreds of people around."

"Not as many as at World Fest, but the picnic was crowded nonetheless."

"Self-defense once she learned he was going to murder her?"

"I've never come across that."

"Self-defense?"

"Premeditated self-defense. I hadn't read that she was fearful?"

"I was just speculating. Could it be a suicide made to look like a murder for insurance purposes? An accident."

Percheron spoke.

"You've covered just about everything. You sound like my niece's partner."

"Oh."

"They are both on the force."

"I wasn't thinking..."

"Partners, like you and me."

"Oh," Ash repeated, pleased.

"Her partner wants to be a writer, so he comes up with a lot of ideas."

"Is that bad?"

"No."

"And I'm doing the same thing? Sorry."

"There is nothing to apologize for. All theories are on the table. In that case and in ours. At some point, we will know almost everything, maybe even the why. Who and why are reflections in a darkened mirror, someone once told me."

"What does that mean?"

"I have no idea. Unlike you, I was hesitant to question everything at the time."

Percheron took a deep breath and then said, "They asked me to stop by and speak with the wife."

Ash said nothing but his face showed both disappointment and curiosity.

Percheron hastened to add, "It was a ten-minute conversation. We are not on the case. I am not on the case, you are not on the case, we are not on the case. Not yet at least."

"What did the wife say?"

Percheron thought of the brief interview before he recounted its contents to Ash.

"You had no guards?"

"I can't speak for everyone, but if we need guards at a temple picnic, well," she trailed off, and Percheron saw, not for the first time, the sequence of thoughts that was running through this middle-aged woman's mind. They were the same as the five stages of any death, beginning with denial.

Her eyes filled with regret. Recognition that guards were required and guilt that she should have known that earlier. She was educated and she considered herself sufficiently sophisticated. In seconds she reached acceptance.

This was the time for Percheron to be his most empathetic and simultaneously cold and calculating. He would question her now, for by the end of the hour, this woman would have moved beyond acceptance into rejection. He had seen it before among the religious; at the end they felt cheated with their celestial bargain. There would be two deaths as a result of the fete: the dead man, and this woman's faith.

"Was your husband religious?" he had asked."

"No more than normal."

"Was that a yes or no?" Ash queried.

Percheron shrugged. Ash decided to ask Perch his thoughts later, in the car. Answers in vehicles were usually more truthful. Was the car a confessional, or were people more open when confined?

"Anyone could have put the poison in his drink, Ash. Including the victim. He was not in the best of health."

Ash nodded, having heard of the victim's medical issues.

"Stroke, kidney failure, three months of dialysis, repeated urinary tract infections. Does physical therapy count as an illness?" Ash asked rhetorically.

# CHAPTER EIGHT

Eddy sat quietly in a pew, replaying mentally the news he had heard on the radio, a dead doctor. While his death by all official accounts was at this point a dreadful accident, no one was able to explain how being poisoned at a picnic was accidental. It was a few days after the doctor's demise, with interest in the case having had time to sprout. It was odd how a story was born, and then seemed to search for the water and light of publicity to survive. The cemetery murder case appeared to have itself been already buried.

It was stranger still that the press was not yet in full gallop on the case. Perhaps they were understaffed or fearful of being sued.

Reporters were paid to connect dots. It was of no consequence if the dots aren't connectable. Rumor, innuendo, alcohol induced dreams; they were equally valid crayons to connect dots. Eddy really missed the gutter press.

An accident?

Eddy knew otherwise. He had played enough sophisticated online games to recognize that a new, subtle play had opened in town. And while this death, murder, he was certain, had been committed in Scene II, there had been another earlier, the body under the tarp in Scene I.

A serial murderer. Someone. Was it himself?

Eddy had a sudden thought and laughed aloud, unconcerned to be chuckling in a synagogue. The building was empty.

Earlier in the week Lewellyn's service had overflowed the cathedral downtown. Grief, both genuine and media induced poured onto the sidewalk and then onto Fifth street itself.

Some commented that larger churches further east could have better accommodated the huge crowd, over twice the size that morbid optimists anticipated. But those buildings were run by other denominations.

Still, it demonstrated that large numbers of believers still attended church, validating Eddy's choice.

Eddy frowned deeply and spoke to the vacant seat beside him.

"Is that the best you can do? You decided that I was not worth a burning bush or an angelic envoy?

Omnipresent? My ass. Omniabsent if you ask me. But you won't, you are in ghost mode, now and forever."

He believed now more than ever, fervently beyond feverishly in its power, in the fetish of one deity, himself.

These legions of middlemen, meddlemen is more apt. They acted as reverse agents, skimming their tax-free percentage, but never once, without exception, not failing to deliver the Talent on site.

They were worse than frauds, their performance more acute than any Ponzi, for those scoundrels provided the goods occasionally, frequently enough to maintain the show. There was a star to be seen.

But here, it was only an empty theatre, no special effects, only the harsh, stony echo of one's voice.

How long does one wait for the biggest of blind dates before accepting that it was a bust? And then, move on to...what?

Another victim? Who would it be? He consulted his written list; one he had committed to memory. He carried it only to remind him that the game was real.

He studied the list again, then rotated it in his hands like an incomprehensible abstract painting. It provided tangible evidence of the game. The game was IRL but suffered from a distinct lack of props.

Life's deficiencies were a constant disappointment. He would do what he could to remedy that deficiency.

He could carry a gun, but half of Kentucky already did that. Something small and quiet. Everyone ported either a 9mm or 40? People lacked imagination.

"How many carried a murder list?" he asked himself. A few, he concluded. Were they playing the same game as him? There were disadvantages to this game, but --- whatever.

He regarded his holy surroundings, comparing them to the others that had served as disappointing waiting rooms. This was the most austere, nothing to see, no place to be awed. He would not wait more than a few minutes longer.

A waiting room, that was the perfect word. One could remain here forever in this large silent space, waiting until Hades, real or imagined, froze over.

The innumerable temples, mosques, and churches formed a network that rivaled that of the nation's airports. Staffed by uncompromising TSA types, preached to and further directed by anonymous voices amplified by electronic speakers, fleeced by numerous tithes, the weary accommodated themselves to the process, while those of sufficient strength elected to minimize their time dreaming of serenity in the clouds and instead drove themselves.

There were so many intermediaries between man and divinity; surely the vast flock of shepherds itself needed shearing. It was a scheme, taking its logo from the residence of long dead pharaohs.

They should have quitted God, left Him behind in his numerous chateaux in the Old World. Instead, they had transported scriptures across oceans with as little thought to consequences as air pollution or fentanyl.

Eddy was on the verge of leaving, counting down silently from one hundred, when he was startled by the sound of the side door opening. It was a nondescript woman, her head covered. Likely a cleaning woman, Eddy speculated. She walked toward him but stopped far enough away that he could not distinguish her features. Her face was in shadow, so she could have been of any age. He considered approaching her but realized that he had nothing to say to her or anyone. Her presence here only accentuated the emptiness of the building.

The Jewish Community center nearby held plays that Eddy had attended. The facility was unattractive in all aspects. There was talk of a new center. Whatever its design, it could not exceed the hideousness of the current facility.

Both buildings were filled with surveillance cameras. He wondered if they were nonoperational, a perfect symbol of an equally inattentive god. He supposed not, the world was a dangerous place with or without a loving deity.

Eddy. He could hear nothing from the silent electronics. He had been told that God laughed at his creations, that was the actual reason for the universe's existence, one large private joke. Eddy heard nothing in the house of worship, no admonishment, no snickering, no laughter. It was the peaceful silence of white noise, so quiet that he imagined he could her the woman breathing.

He turned and left, leaving the stranger in the solitude that he no longer found welcoming. He was disappointed but not discouraged, he thought, tapping the list, neatly folded in the breast pocket of his shirt.

He was in character, his character was genuine, all else was stage. His antagonist had failed to show, and had not the courtesy to send an understudy, or even a brief text. There was no going back. This was the correct rendezvous, the printed copy of the victim's obituary rested in his rear pants pockets. He consulted it again to be sure; yes, there was no mistake. His costar was absent, but he, Eddy would carry one.

Eddy's car ascended the slight ramp to the freeway, quickly attaining highway speed as he headed East, the traditional direction of deities, leaving behind all false signs. He exited soon thereafter, deciding to take the back way home.

The trees along Springdale were of middle-aged girth. They were long time sedentary, not massive, but thick enough to stop the most distracted of persons at the wheel of a speeding car. Was it altruistic worry for the passing stranger, or was it human selfishness that accounted for the warnings affixed to the rough texture of the bark?

The signs were crude, simple, from all indications fabricated by the hands of children, and for those that reason undoubtedly effective. If the fluttering of leaves did not trap one's attention, the adolescent tableaux were the next defense, backed next by the strong, well-rooted living columns of wood that served as the final physical barrier against collision with one of the nearby houses, presumably inhabited by a young artist. Beyond the leaves, beyond the signs, past the trees, lay luck.

Eddy was tempted to fling dice, to twist and release the steering wheel, to treat it as if it was roulette, but by the time he had reached a decision point and had begun to modify his grasp, he had passed through the child safe zone.

The world was more than a stage. It was a beautiful, ugly game. It was a game; he would improve it. He had been stood up for the last time.

It was larping, and cosplay and GTA all in one.  He was no longer playing in the world, the world would play in his existence.

# CHAPTER NINE

The following day, the bright sunlight warmed and sprouted Eddy's regrets. He was embarrassed, the activities of the day before as unforgiveable as those he had probably committed during the alcoholic blackouts that were occurring more and more frequently.

Eddy returned to the synagogue. It was empty as it had been yesterday when he had arrived.

As if in a dream, he sat in the same seat, and again a few minutes later a door opened and in walked a woman. No, it was not a woman but an old man.

The man took a seat near Eddy.

"Well, this was something," Eddy thought.

"I have an appointment."

Eddy had no idea what that meant. The comment was as expected as it was unexpected.

"It's flexible."

The game had been going on for only a few days, yet it seemed to have been part of Eddy's entire existence. There was the game, and there was him, and there existed, maybe, the other player. The one who had started this activity which was now the center of his self. Sometimes he hoped that the other was him, for then they would never lose each other, and the game could continue until they both wearied of it.

Eddy sensed that the man expected some sort of response, a few words, more than just a nod acknowledging his presence.

He decided to hedge his bet.

"Have you been to Paristown?"

"No. I've never been out of the country. They have beautiful sights in Paris, I hear. Have you been there yourself and seen them?"

"No, I haven't," Eddy lied as a test.

"That makes two of us."

Eddy was still unsure of the man, puzzled by his arrival, annoyed by his seat selection. What did he want? Surely this was pure happenstance.

The stranger replied as if he had surmised Eddy's thoughts.

"I've been told by a doctor. I'll die."

"I am sorry to hear that."

"Thanks. That makes two of us," he repeated.

"I come here when I don't feel well."

Eddy nodded.

"It's a clean, quiet place in the shade to die. What do you think?"

"I agree."

"Good. That makes two of us."

Eddy sat there for a few more minutes and then stood, nodded, and left without saying a word.

Nor did the stranger. That made two of them.

Eddy was grateful for the warmth of the day. He was nearly shivering. It was stupid. But sometimes stupid was fun. And necessary. Fools were rarely correct, but no one is wrong all the time.

# CHAPTER TEN

The text arrived like a crying newborn. Kimberly scanned its contents and smiled. She had a date for tomorrow, a lunch date. Those were the best as they offered alternatives. Eddy, that sounded like an ok name. She wondered if he too might be a keeper. When it rains, it pours, she thought, even in July. Raining men.

Kimberly considered her friend, the well-known murder mystery author Annacine Finley. Annacine knew how to retain a man but had forgotten how to catch one. For Kimberly it was just the opposite. The real world was harder than it read.

"Annacine should write her new book about me," Kimberly decided. Instead, her friend was writing a low priority book, a Christmas book. By low priority Annacine meant that she had written the story in 20 minutes, plot and ending complete. It needed expansion, as three hundred words did not constitute a marketable product.

Annacine should stick to murder, Kimberly had advised. She would have restated her opinion if she had been asked again.

It had become a joke between the two of them although Kimberly wondered recently if she was the butt of it.

Annacine spoke of the Christmas story now and again. It was part religious, part science fiction.

Kimberly despised both as equally fanciful. They were two of a kind, one with less interesting characters. Christmas, she thought and shivered despite the heat. The holiday revived bad memories and she was not in the mood to relive anything associated with that season.

She liked Annacine better when she stuck to murder. She recalled one conversation in particular.

"People overreact to murder; they treat is with such drama and seriousness."

"Of course they do! How else should they behave?"

"They should behave better. That is all I know. They have no expectation of living forever. Is murder the worst way to die? Murder is human passion at its most intense. We all die. Murder is simply an option, like which movie to see."

Kimberly's thoughts returned to tomorrow. She would have options. Lunch, and then options.


"I thought that we could have lunch in Nulu. Is that ok with you, Kimberly?" Eddy said.

"Sure, Eddy" Kimberly replied, self-conscious that she sounded like a teenager when she was anything but that. Eddy was younger than she had thought, but then she had not asked his age. Men had no perfect age, whereas a woman's age was always perfect.

As they exited on Third street, Eddy looked over and said,

"We are early, I'd like to make a short detour. We will still be on time."

Kimberly did not like the unexpected alteration but said nothing. It was only when they pulled into the parking lot that she relaxed.

"This must be the shortest courtship in history. But it's going to end sadly for you."

"What?"

"You haven't even brought a ring, I suppose? I have expensive tastes."

She saw the perplexity on his face.

"I'm joking. About the ring. Not my tastes. Seriously, why are we here Eddy?"

"I hope to meet someone here."

"Don't we all." She paused. "A friend?"

"No, not a friend."

He said as one expert in not having friends.

Kimberly shivered. They were parked under the shade provided by a large tree, and the air conditioner was set to max cold.

She reached to adjust the temperature, but at that moment, her companion pressed the off button.

The engine stopped and the frigid air ceased.

"An acquaintance."

"That is preferable to a hastily arranged wedding," Kimberly teased.

"Should I wait here?" she asked politely, knowing that he'd have left the car running if that was the case. She laughed at her own silliness.

"What's funny?"

"Nothing. I was thinking..."

"There is no sense in waiting here. It will be uncomfortable in a few minutes."

And he is afraid to leave me unattended the keys or the car running, she thought. Religious people can be so distrusting. They know from personal experience how bad one can be, so they run to a god to tell them their behavior is ok.

She could sense him waiting. Or maybe he is just a cheap greenie, sacrificing her physical comfort in order to rescue the planet.

He blushed, realizing the reason for Kimberly's hesitancy.

He exited the vehicle, stepped around the rear of the car, and stopped beside her, opening the passenger door with a "Sorry. I'm out of practice."

As they walked to the church she spoke.

"I've been the victim of a hastily arranged wedding. It didn't work out better than the others. It's funny."

"What is, Kimberly?"

"Girls dream of their wedding day. I must have too, don't you think? Do men?" she asked, her voice devoid of curiosity.

"I don't think so," Eddy replied, piqued by the unusual question.

"But now, nightly visits of weddings and chapels are the opening scenes of nightmares for me. Its maybe better to just pretend that one is married."

"Really?" Eddy asked, fascinated by Kimberly's philosophy.

"Really. Lies make for comfortable pajamas."

"I never thought of lies that way."

"I can't envision them any other way. I have an entire wardrobe."

As they entered the nave, Kimberly warned, "This had better not be a drug deal. The church is too beautiful for such a tawdry transaction."

They took the first available pew, which was the first as the building was empty except for them.

After a moment, Kimberly said,

"There are so many flowers. There must have been a wedding here earlier."

"Or a funeral. If he doesn't show in five minutes we will leave."

"Your friend, I mean your acquaintance doesn't seem reliable."

"He has flaked on me before."

"Are we supposed to sit here quietly and wait for a flake?"

They sat quietly for a minute, both keenly aware of the oddness of the situation.

Kimberly picked up a prayer book from the slot in the back of the pew, then replaced it.

"Reading the same book your entire existence? Does that strike you as evidence of a simple mind? Or as proof of a mind at all?"

"Do you believe in God?"

"Any and all except yours."

"You don't like to share?"

"I don't wear hand me downs. Not anymore. I live my own life, and don't let others bleed into it.

"You have a strong will."

Kimberly smiled.

"How else could I make it to cardio mashup class at 0540 three days a week?"

Eddy thought, "That is about when I'm getting to bed. He disliked being sober, knowing that when he woke, that was going to be the best that he would feel all that day."

Silence again descended.

"If you are interested there are a few saints in those glass cases near the altar."

"Really," he added in response to her facial expression.

For the next few minutes, Eddy pondered, while Kimberly walked up front to see if Eddy had been teasing her.

He had brought Kimberly along as either a witness or as a secondary affront, this one female. Ironically, she was safe from himself. Any smiting of Kimberly Fredrichs would not be his doing.

Casting into fire, smiting, or turning to salt, he was waiting.

"Nada," he thought after a few minutes of diminishing expectations.

"Five minutes," he said aloud a moment later, posing it as a challenge to anyone within earshot."

"You've been ghosted."

"As I expected. He has done this before."

After a moment, Eddy asked "Do you think I'm stupid?"

His companion laughed.

"Do you?"

"Telling someone they're stupid doesn't increase their intelligence, it makes them angry and determined."

"Besides," she added, "I don't know you well enough to answer all your questions. Your contact ghosted you. Your two anorexics in their cases have not raised a bony finger to help. You can sit here and wait for Godot, but I much prefer that you take me to lunch before some clergy man measures me for one of those glass booths."

"There is no one here."

"Exactly my point. Although I half expected a film crew or someone to pop out of the glass casket. You enjoy games."

"You know who I am?"

She looked puzzled at his question.

"I know a boy when I meet one. So far this is one memorable first date, and I use the term extremely loosely. I feel confident now that I'll live to be available for a second one."

Eddy laughed.

"God, I'm glad your friend slash acquaintance was a no show. God only knows what happened to him. God, he isn't a woman, is he?"

"You act as if there is no god."

"And you act as if there is nothing except god. So what? Religion is a slow rolling cult movie, where everyone has learned the lines so well that they believe the plot.

Whoever you codenamed god missed an appointment. He can reschedule. After lunch."

"I did not intend that as an insult, Kim."

"Was it intended as a manly observation?"

"No. It was not an observation, manly or otherwise. I meant it as a compliment."

"Oh?"

"I admire you. You act as if there is no God."

"You already said that."

"Yes, I did. And God acts as if there is no us."

"Is there an us? You move fast. I'm still hungry. Like I said, your no-show can reschedule."

"Lunch?"

"God yes.  Oops, He's back in the conversation.  If we make it a super long lunch..."

"Yes?"

"I was going to suggest dancing, but it would still be too early.  I'm not one to disrespect decorum, particularly since none of the good clubs are open.'

"And the bad clubs?"

"They never reopen."

"Lunch it is then."

As they walked the short way down the aisle, Eddy commented,

"You enjoy playing with matches."

"Matchsticks are for little boys.  My brother, for instance.  As for me, I prefer bonfires."

"You must love Burning Man."

"Burning Men? Some of them deserve it."

A moment later, Kim added. "

"If you're in doubt, leave a note.  Some people have issues with time.  Others are like my laptop.  Once I turn it on, it refuses to stop telling me what to do.  It suggests this and that, but never recommends that I simply unplug it."

"Forget the note, maybe we'll meet later elsewhere," Eddy answered.  He did not add that he was a full-time resident of doubt.


"What do you do for fun?" Kimberly asked, as they waited for their meal.

"Whatever I want."

"That must be wonderful."

"Yeah, it must be," he said in a way that implied it was less than wonderful.

He looked at her as if she had just asked the question and he had not yet answered.

"Wonderful," Kimberly thought, sensing Eddy's hesitation, "a man who reconsiders."

"It is wonderful. Wonderful, wonderful." His words rang out, with an emotion that Eddy was unaccustomed to.

He laughed and Kimberly relaxed for the first time with him. Laughs are truth detectives she had convinced herself long ago, after numerous false starts.

"But enough about me," Eddy said. "Tell me about yourself."

"Better and better," Kimberly thought.

# CHAPTER ELEVEN

The middle-aged female walker saw the man approaching on the narrow park path, visibly puffing as he ascended the trail that sloped downward in the direction she was moving. He stopped suddenly next to a bench but instead of sitting down, he reached in his pocket and bent over slightly, his attention focused on the shrubbery to his right.

Alert, the woman tensed, concerned but not fearful. Her mood changed when she saw what the stranger did next. He tossed something on the ground, peanuts. He had stopped to feed a rabbit.

It was as good an excuse as any, she thought to herself, noticing that the man was still gathering his breath. He must have worked his whole life, and his body had to wait, she concluded.

"You are so good to feed them," she said to the man.

Hunger overcame caution and the hare approached the peanuts that had been spread on the walking trail and began devouring them. The man and woman stood quietly for a minute, watching the small herbivore, which was now actively ignoring them.

Its unexpected meal finished, the rabbit hopped slowly away, and the man stood silently as it departed. He then seated himself on the bench and relaxed, and listened to the cicadas, he and the rabbit both content with the morning.

The women murmured goodbye before continuing her circuit of the park.

A few paces later, before she entered a tree lined section, she turned back for a final look at the peaceful scene, then faced forward again, and continued her walk down the sloping asphalt trail.

A brief fifteen minutes later the woman completed her circuit and was not surprised to observe the man still in the same place. The rabbit was nowhere to be seen. She stopped before him and parted her lips, as if to restart their previous conversation, but she said nothing. A trail of semi congealed blood ran from the dead man's mouth to his left shoulder, descending toward, but petering out before it reached his left hand, which still clutched the small paper sack containing a few remaining peanuts.

Eddy ran. He was a runner. He was running. The word reverberated in his head, lap after lap. This was today's first lap, made difficult by the remnants of alcohol in his body. He pictured it flowing through his heart, his arteries and veins, its transparency lightening slightly the crimson of the blood in which it rode.

Each morning, he swore off alcohol, but welcomed it back into his life each evening. Sometimes in the afternoon.

Lap after lap, he and the alcohol would run concentric circles, the booze unthinking, himself unable to not think, thinking far too much. Concentric excessivity, that was it.

61

He thought of his game, of the recent murders. Of the ones he knew would occur. Life and fantasy were beginning to combine. He was completing his first lap, begun at the bench where the older man sat. Before the man stood a woman of the same age. His wife, Eddy surmised.

Eddy had passed the man earlier, silently mocking his lack of conditioning. He could have been another victim, easily attacked. Eddy visualized the assault, a quick stab with the knife he had taken to carrying as protection on his runs and then tossing the body over the bridge into the creek below. Or not. The man was heavy. Simpler to stab the overweight, huffing man and continue his run as if nothing had happened. That is what he could have done.

Instead, alcohol had intervened, to his benefit for once, forcing Eddy into the public toilet to retch and otherwise eject the excesses of the night before, feeling as if he himself were victim rather than assailant.

Who was he to ridicule the chubby stranger? he had thought in a moment of contrition.

Eddy's attention was drawn by a flash of movement. A coyote was crossing the lower pasture of the park, with a glance over his shoulder that was part fearful of Eddy and part an appraisal of Eddy as a potential meal. Eddy was glad that he had protection.

The woman noticed Eddy's approach, stepped from the narrow path onto the grass, and began to scream.

Eddy stopped near the couple and felt for his knife, unsure of the situation, further confused when he realized that his weapon was gone. Had he dropped it, forgotten it? He felt as if he were half asleep, watching an old video of his childhood, a scene once familiar yet strange.

He chuckled without cause and the woman glanced at him nervously, a hair trigger pull away from screaming again.

The man looked ill, very ill.

Eddy felt again for his knife and regretted the movement instantly. The knife was not there, he carried it for protection, yet at this moment he was grateful for his forgetfulness. Or was it alcohol amnesia?

"Are you his wife?" he asked as a way of countering his furtive movement.

"No, I'm not. He's been stabbed. In the back. Who are you? Call the police." The words came in three-word bursts.

"Now, young man. Call the police!" she commanded.

Her phrases were simple, concise, firm. Eddy turned and ran to the building that served as administration and scheduling of the numerous tennis courts that lay within the park grounds.

## CHAPTER TWELVE

"I could be a suspect."

"We get that question a lot, sir."

"It is not a question. I'd have a good chance of skating on one murder."

"Is that a confession?" Perch asked jokingly.

"I said one murder, but not several."

"So..."

"So nothing. This is not a confession, simply an observation."

"Why several?"

"Two detectives? For a murder in Lime Kiln? I don't frequent that part of town. I don't rub elbows with that sort."

"Which sort is that?"

"The sort that has two detectives assigned to their murder."

"So..."

Robert paused, waiting to see if the young detectives sang more than one note. He didn't.

"So you must be assigned to that case, but you are here to see me about something else. So," he grinned at his interrogators, "there must be another murder. Possibly related. If it wasn't related to Lime Kiln, someone else on your team would be here instead of you two."

"We are short staffed today," the young detective lied.

"What else makes you think we have several murders?"

"I read the papers."

"And?"

Robert smiled slightly at the new note.

"What do the papers say?" Perch added.

"It is what the papers don't say. Folks like those, the ones who have died recently, aren't murdered. You have done a great job of portraying this as a series of accidents, suicides, random crime."

"There are streaks, coincidences."

"If you believe that, you may need to bring a third detective onboard. What about that female detective?"

An image of Castorina leapt into Perch's mind.

"She's on vacation."

"Don't worry, I won't say anything."

"I am grateful if you don't," Perch said sincerely.

"Do you have a few minutes to talk about your nephew?"

"Eddy?"

"Yes. Excuse me for saying so, but you mentioned Eddy immediately."

"I don't have any other nephews."

Perch was reminded again how much he disliked intelligent witnesses, especially when the witness was also a suspect.

"Just when I'd concluded that he was an ok guy, I discovered that he had bought himself a BMW. A new one."

The detectives nodded in unison as way of encouragement.

"I used to have a suit for every day of the week. Now, I have one for every funeral. The same one of course. No one remarks on my lack of wardrobe."

The uncle relished his first complaint of the day. It went so well with coffee.

"You are retired, Mr. Burnell?"

He nodded yes.

"I thought about, still do in fact, a part time job. But when I think about working with today's public... Horrible! My thoughts turn to shooting someone again."

The detectives were taken aback.

"Again?" one said, as the two men took a step back in tandem.

Eddy's uncle laughed at their discomfort.

"I say again, only because I wanted to shoot some of my so-called clients when I was working."

He laughed again.

"You two sure are jumpy. You need to cut down on your caffeine intake."

Was this uncle of Eddy's present his own soon to be future, Perch wondered.

"You should be careful about what you say, Mr. Burnell," Ash advised.

"I don't care what you think. I don't care what I think. Thinking is overrated."

They stood there quietly, tense.

"You have questions about my nephew." It was not posed as a question.

"What makes you think that?"

"Don't be coy. It looks creepy on men. I know creepy."

"Your nephew? Is he creepy?"

"No."

"I'm surprised that you mentioned Eddy without my asking."

"You are here asking questions. It can't be about me, as I'm not interesting to the police or anyone else. It must be Eddy by process of elimination."

"What about the creeps?"

"The police don't need to ask me or anyone else about them. You can pick them up by the dozen in any city ward. And it doesn't need a detective."

"Tell us about Eddy."

"He's interesting."

"In what way?"

"In the way that I'm not. Don't misunderstand me. He isn't all that. Compared to me, you are probably as interesting as Eddy. I'm a low bar. You know, a low bar is not a bad position to be in."

"Eddy," the detective prompted as he feared that the uncle was ready to detail the boring life of a low bar.

"He is a dreamer."

"A player?"

"Not in the sense you probably mean it. He doesn't rise to that level. Player used to be a compliment, in a half-assed way. He is a player. A kid like so many of these boys today. They don't think of themselves as men, so why should I?"

"Would you call him immature?"

"Have you met Eddy?"

The detective nodded yes.

"Then you have your answer. You are paid by the hour. And so you are out here asking silly questions."

Burnell sighed.

"He plays. He is a player. He plays games that strangers create. All the kids, all the boys do. They play, and play, and they never stop playing. If I was smart, I'd have figured out one of the games. Better yet, I should have created one myself and made a fortune too. But..." His thoughts drifted off.

"A criminal?"

"He lacks inertia to be a criminal. Eddy has barely enough energy to be a witness. It's those games that I spoke of."

"Criminals should be put down."

"Your own nephew?"

"If he was criminal," Percheron added.

"I have others."

"You do?"

"Yeah. A few, somewhere out west. In places without clouds. Eddy is the only one who comes around."

"For money?"

"It helps."

The detective raised his eyebrows. The money flowed in the other direction, he realized.

"That is the problem with men like Eddy, they never stop playing. Eddy is smart, he could design another game. But he is like the others."

Percheron knew Eddy better than his uncle did. Eddy was no basement gamer.

"In what way?"

"Lazy. Dreamers. They imagine they are someone else, anyone other than themselves. It's crazy. It is such a waste of life."

"A waste of life?" Ash interjected.

"Of time. That is life. And when they fail, they call it getting bored, they respawn or move on to another game. It is all so foolish. Respawn."

"You are the second person to use that word recently."

"I won't be the last. They excel at failing at games. Games are practice for life. That should tell them something, don't you think? They won't consider playing life as themselves instead of a fantasy as a goofy character.

Eddy had a good job, a real career. But he saw that as a means to play games. You know, how a boy earns money mowing lawns and then blows it on a toy. You are supposed to learn that lesson quickly."

"He quit?"

"To be fair, he made a bunch of money in investments. I remember he called it day trading stonks or some such crap. I thought it was another game, but guys at the bar explained it to me.

Stonks, are a sort of high-tech stock, whatever the hell that is. It struck me as some stupid." Burnell stopped speaking without finishing the sentence.

"Oh well, it's his life. He doesn't criticize mine. It annoys me all the same that he is spending his life as a reflection of a stranger's imaginary creation. He needs to play his own life, where he makes the rules. These players are in some childish cult. It is as demanding as some crazy religion."

"Does Eddy have friends?"

"Eddy involved? He doesn't involve himself."

"In what?"

"He does, he did ok with his work. I never understood it so there is no use asking. Computers something or other. It was work, then those online games. Or maybe the games came first. It makes no difference now does it? It's all computers and now they tell us what to do."

The man noticed the detective's quick scan of his abode. He invited them inside.

"You won't find one here. I may be crazy, but not insane. Crazy is a sign of wisdom. Sometimes," he rebutted himself.

"Where is the woman detective?"

The question was unexpected and remained unanswered.

"By the hour like I said," Burnell said with disgust.

"The hell with it," he said, half turning away.

"Is Eddy religious?"

The uncle guffawed, not deigning to look over his shoulder in response.

"God doesn't have a presence on the internet."

"Do you know anything about where Eddy was?"

"We had breakfast the other day. That's it."

"You have no children yourself?"

"I was afraid to have children, so I didn't. I was afraid to make too much money, so I didn't. I was afraid to congratulate myself on my success, so I didn't."

"Why?"

"You have to ask?"

"I don't understand. I ask. It has become who I am," Percheron said as way of explanation.

"I was afraid that it could all be taken away. I wanted to escape God."

"Escape God?"

"Escape His notice. It sounds ridiculous when I say it aloud. It didn't work."

"What do you mean by that? What didn't work?"

"Life, so drab without death," Percheron reflected to himself.

"I have enough money and enough years to not let myself be jerked around."

"You look poor to me."

"I have a rich nephew."

"It doesn't show," the detective remarked, making a point to look around slowly at the home which was bested described as fraying.

"You don't like people much."

"I don't like people period. "

Percheron picked up a book from the bare coffee table, *Constructing belief in the modern age*

"This looks well read."

"I bought it in Carmichael's bookstore. Its rubbish, but it makes an excellent coaster. What case are you working on?"

Perch spoke for them both.

"We usually ask the awkward questions."

"House rules men," he said firmly, then with a relenting grin added, "Fire away."

He leaned back into the worn chair, whose days of being overstuffed were over. He closed his eyes.

"Ask your questions," he commanded, sensing but not seeing their puzzled expressions.

"Where were you on July 7 between the hours,"

His full smile halted the query.

"Really? Where was I on July 7? I have no frigging clue. Probably here. I am here most days. I could check my schedule or review my surveillance cameras, but I haven't gotten around to having either. Does it matter? You could check my cell phone records, but..." he trailed off.

"We are working, Mr. Burnell."

"Murder, accident, suicide? Three flavors of a cold ice cream that no one finds delicious.

What I remember clearly detective is a recent dream. My pet frog was killed today. Just a dream. Don't particularly care for frogs. He escaped to death in the ocean. I followed him down in time to see him eaten by a shark. It was purely my imagination, attachment to something completely fabricated."

"Maybe the frog was symbolic."

Burnell shrugged.

"Dreams are crap."


Eddy's uncle had his own name. It was not impressive. The rich and the poor of the planet staked out the largest, outlandish territory where exotic names flourished.

The name Robert Burnell was not among them. His nickname, Bob, did not add to the weight of the moniker.

"I remember what I remember, what," said the man with the forgettable name.

72

Yet the comment, with its odd Britishism, sparked a memory in the mind of Percheron. It reminded him of some other case, vague, long ago.

Not so much of a case, but a trial.

A witness had used that exact phrase, "I remember what I remember, what" and Percheron would not have recalled it except for the verbal exchange that had followed, between that witness and the defense attorney.

The attorney had questioned the accuracy of the witness' memory. The witness, was it this same man, thirty years later, had won the contest by saying,

"If someone asks me in six months, what I remember about you, and I answer that you are an arrogant fool, would I be remembering correctly?"

The courtroom had erupted in laughter, and the witness had been excused with no more questions.

Percheron wondered why he had been in the courtroom that day. Whatever the case was, it had not been his. Maybe he had stepped in to get in out of the cold or heat of the day. A murder case?

The cases he did not work were jumbled together, tragedy as background, while his own were crystal clear, the edges still sharp.

"I remember what I remember, what?" Percheron repeated mentally. It was a coincidence that might blossom into a genuine lead. He would follow the hunch and see of Robert (Bob) Burnell had been a witness for the prosecution, in an unknown case, twenty-five or thirty years ago.

Or he could simply ask the man who stood before him today.

"We are done here, Mr. Burnell," he heard Ash say, bringing the moment to a decision point. Ash looked questioningly at his partner, who nodded, and added, "Thanks for your time."

"He knows too much, but not enough," Percheron said as they returned to their car.

# CHAPTER THIRTEEN

Later, as he drove home, the older detective remembered another sentence that Burnell had uttered that could have been spoken by himself: "I wake up tired."

Percheron was not happy with this unexpected newcomer to his long list of murderers.

"Society was changing, face it," he said aloud. It had changed. He felt himself playing a game where all had changed, except the uniforms. It was unsettling, a sensation made worse by the fear that his young colleagues were as unaware of the new world, as he himself had been until recently. He could do nothing at this stage in his career. Percheron was tired.

The crime was neither more repulsive nor more compelling than others but is was certainly more public.

It was bold, apparently senseless but the very word senseless had lost what meaning it once held.

The vaunted causes of crime, the unholy trinity of booze, broads, and bucks, had to make space for this chaotic disruptor.

Mentioning this would serve no purpose, either for his colleagues or himself. Or for the victims' families. There had to be meaning in every action, didn't there? Perhaps he was wrong, and his approaching end date had turned him bitter. Only this case and the next one, and the ones after mattered, until... Until.

The immediate concern was his conviction that the park murder was another in a series. He would mention it to Ash, soon, and they would come up with an innocuous term, he noticed the plate on the car in front, yes, case 4802 would do, innocuous as any other number, one that would provide no clue to a journalist.

He rolled slowly by the homes in his neighborhood, house by house, cognizant of the 25-mph speed limit, a restriction not blasted by flashing lights that scolded without end.

Each brick mailbox he crawled past stood as witness, enumerated like a tombstone, providing equally little information to the passerby or visitor, as to the inhabitants temporarily constrained to life.

He turned right, pulling into his private plot.

# CHAPTER FOURTEEN

"The woman is mysterious."

"She would be. Aren't they all?" Ash replied.

"She is our only witness," Percheron stated.

"Is she? Why is that?" he continued. "There were other people in the park. It's popular with walkers and runners and tennis players."

"The tennis ladies arrived later," Ash reminded Percheron. "Our witness was the first to report the murder."

"That isn't entirely correct. She had no phone. Eddy what's his name, the same. No phone. I find that an odd coincidence."

"Eddy claimed he was going to run to the office to call us, but he hesitated to leave the woman alone. He said he was concerned for her with a killer about. And he said he did not want to leave the body unattended."

"Do you find it odd that neither had a cell phone with them? Who doesn't carry a phone? Hell, even I carry one. A young, healthy man, running? Sure? But Emerald?"

"What a name, huh?"

"She is none of the above."

"She claimed that she left it in the car. She said that she was worried about radio waves causing cancer."

"She fears that more than a mugger in the park?"

"It was a bright morning. Would you be worried about a mugger?"

"Yes, if I were her."

"She carries a whistle instead."

"Did she use it?"

"I don't think so. She might not have had time."

"Let's ask her. And then ask Eddy. Ask everyone who was at the park."

"If they heard a whistle?"

"Yes".

"Is it important?" Ash asked.

Percheron shrugged.

"I should have thought to ask them the day of the murder. Oh well, it's good to have a reason to interview them again."

The assistant hurriedly asked another question. In his haste he uttered the words before realizing how improbable they were.

"Do you think that Eddy and Emerald killed him together? Never mind. I'm tired."

"What was your reason for joining the police Ash?"

"You will have to wait until I come up with one. I used to wonder why I did anything. You read for a part and the director chooses you for a completely different role."

"You've done theatre?"

"In college."

The expected slight did not come.

"Six months on the job convinced me that hardly anyone has a clue why they do what they do.

It took me over a year. But then, I'm not as smart as you," the judgement delivered without sarcasm.

The young man felt himself back at an audition, once again uncertain of both his role and lines. Having no script, he ad libbed.

"I guess the devil made me do it, explains it as well as a grand design."

Later, the young man, replayed the conversation in his mind, before he fell asleep. Perhaps his subconscious would derive a deeper message from Percheron's words, for his conscious brain had been unsuccessful. So much for his superior intellect.

"Why did you join the force?"

"I wanted a job without stress and then I settled for this one. I also wanted a job where I was home nights."

"Right."

"It was either this or driving truck. Police came up heads."

"Do you regret your choice?"

"I kept the half dollar, thinking I might go two out of three with myself.

Solving these crimes is not a contest among us. It's a battle between us, all of us, against him. What it is not us, I mean us, you and me, against other cops. My career, such as it is, is over. Credit goes to the entire team." Percheron hesitated.

"I hope we solve this."

"Our chances?"

"Good. I'm aware that you have your own career to consider. We will get him."

Percheron was silent for a long moment.

"The odds are in our favor. The numbers are in our favor, technology is in our favor. But..."

"But?"

"Fortune favors the evil."

"Not the bold?"

"Two sides of the same coin more often than not."

"Like your Kennedy half?"

"It's a Franklin. We have the best job in the world, except maybe doctors. We experience life as it actually is. It surpasses those video games I've heard of."

His partner smiled at the idea of Perch playing GTA.

"But it is one hundred percent real. No do overs, no excuses, no silver bullets. Crime solving has gotten easier. But it goes from crime to punishment. We are skipped over. Hell, arrest is not punishment. But J&J believes that it does, and poof, we are back to zero. The judge or jury turns over their card, and its advance directly to Go, do not go to jail, for the defendant."

"Do you regret it?" Ash asked again.

"I have a brother who has lived in regret long enough to run for its mayor. I prefer Louisville."

"I didn't know you had a brother. What does he do?"

"You know the question adults ask children 'What do you want to be when you grow up?'"

Ash nodded.

"For my brother it was nothing. Nothing is not an acceptable answer. For him, growing up was a disappointment. He had to get through, he had to become something before he could finally become nothing. It was a waste, he said to me once, life was just a big circle, without shortcuts. We all become nothing in time, including those who think they are something. Maybe he was correct."

"The things you learn in this job. An arbor antenna," Ash said, returning to the case.

"What's that?"

"Something to do with operating a ham radio. You toss a weight over a high branch and use an attached rope to raise a wire antenna for better reception. The operator was too busy talking with strangers around the country to notice the happenings a hundred yards distant. Everyone saw nothing. Their consistency is in their blindness. No one heard anything, except the ham who was flirting with a woman in Arkansas. No one observed the least oddity. Hell, a missing rabbit is our most promising witness. It is frustrating to the point of absurdity, Perch. We have three sober adults, none with a link to the victim. They have no reason to lie.

And yet all we have is an uncorroborated reference to our own Bugs Bunny. He is the only one with anything resembling a motive and opportunity, but no means, unless rabbits have suddenly acquired skills with bladed instruments.

We are at ground zero, with the damned bunny holed up below."

Perch laughed at the image.

"Suicide?" he suggested facetiously.

"No prints on the handle."

"Oh yeah," he agreed, knowing full well that the blade had been clear of any fingerprints or DNA.

"Cherchez le lapin," he thought, wondering what their next step should be.

"Two strangers meet each other in a park and decide to murder a third stranger and then stand there waiting for a fourth stranger to walk by and do what?"

His speculation was ridiculous, unreasonable, Ash knew but he preserved.

"And the pair remain there until a fourth stranger shows up so they can alert more strangers, us?  Perch, the body could have been dragged away but wasn't. That would have left blood smears on Eddy."

"Eddy?"

"Sure.  He runs a lap as a disguise and returns to 'find  the victim'. Maybe he saw Emerald approaching and improvised.

His embarrassment turned to curiosity when they were told that Emerald was asking to see them.

"Thank you both for seeing me again today, detectives," Emerald said, placing her cellphone in her purse as she took an offered seat.

"I'm glad you stopped by today," Percheron began.

"We were wondering if you had blown your whistle, when..."

"In the park?  No, I didn't.  When the moment came, it just happened so fast.  That young man was approaching, and I thought well, he must be here to help. And.." she trailed off.

Percheron nodded.

"I'm glad I could clear up your question about the whistle.  I have something..."

"Emerald is an odd name."

"As odd as Perch?" Emerald replied flatly.

"His name is Percheron," the younger detective interjected defensively.

"Oh my!"

She looked at the young man with feigned surprise, then turned to Percheron.

"Percheron is nearly as odd."

She faced again the other detective.

"You can't be sensitive on someone's behalf."

"Personal experience?" Perch asked.

"Personal experiences," Emeral confirmed. "I'm a slow learner".

"I doubt that."

"In some things," she said as compromise. "Anyway, odd names are memorable."

"Like Emerald?".

Emerald nodded.

"Did you choose it yourself?"

"I did. Eighteen years after my mother chose Emerald for me, I chose not to correct her. She made few good decisions. You can call me Emy if you like."

"Is that what your friends call you?"

The question came from Perch's colleague, followed by one from Perch.

"What else?"

"About my mother? Well...let me think."

"About the case."

"The case", Emerald repeated somberly. "Such a harsh word, case. Case, it's impossible to say it softly." She tried a few times, in an unsuccessful attempt to refute herself.

"When you first hear of someone's death, their life runs through your mind."

83

"Does it? I thought it was the other way round."

"You do? That would be odd. How would they know whose life.... I must sound silly, I see now what you mean. You are correct."

Percheron interrupted.

"What went through your mind when you realized that the man you had met only minutes before was dead?"

"That is what I was getting to. If you hear of someone's death their life blasts through your mind. But it is blurry, those are the parts you don't see, because you know only a portion of their lives. For close friends, it's still vignettes, clear snatches of a few shared moments or days. It's not life, it's not their life, it's an impression of a life, stored here," she concluded, touching her head with the index finger of her right hand.

The younger detective was reminded of someone visually describing a self-inflicted gunshot.

He looked at Percheron who was himself gazing at the witness.

"You see, I didn't know anything about this man, all that I could picture was the rabbit. I feel useless. If only the rabbit could speak." No one smiled at the remark.

Ash wondered if the woman was in delayed shock.

"The case?" Perch prompted, uttering the word as non-threateningly as he could. Perhaps a whisper would elicit a more valuable response. It had sometimes functioned like a dagger piercing a tire. But today his ploy itself fell flat.

Emerald concentrated for a moment, then responded.

"No detectives. I have nothing to add. It's not like a TV show where I would suddenly recall a critical clue. I have nothing to offer except what I told you that terrible day."

"Do you flirt when you're nervous?" Percheron asked bluntly.

Ash was surprised at the question yet noticed that neither of them blushed. He wondered if he himself had turned red, refusing to confirm it by looking at the mirrored wall.

"It must show to an experienced investigator."

Perch smiled at her parry.

"Yes, I flirt when I'm nervous."

"And when you aren't nervous?" the other male voice asked.

"I flirt much better," she replied simply. It had been a long time since she had played with two single men. "You must think me scattered, behaving this way in such dire circumstances".

Perch smiled again at her arcane phrase.

"This murder has shaken me."

"That's normal", a young voice assured her.

"Louisville is the home of the Kentucky Derby," Emerald said.

The detectives were equally puzzled by this sudden change of subject.

"I moved here too late to attend it. Maybe next year."

"It's nearly a religion. Christmas in May instead of July, the young detective joked. Or December," he added to dead air.

"The Kentucky Derby?" Emerald queried, heaping confusion on the fluttering conversation.

"Yeah, Derby."

"Is it true that once thrown by a horse, you need to remount immediately?"

Ash nodded.

"Yes, assuredly," he proclaimed despite himself never having been astride a saddle.

Emerald nodded in relief.

"That is what I tried," she stated mysteriously.

"I see it over and over, in my dreams. And then I wake and it's over but not over. I think of that rabbit in the park. Will I see him again? He was so friendly. I used to have the best cat. He was a joyous animal, the happiest mammal I've ever seen. God must have taken all the happiness that a dozen humans squandered and squeezed into a kitten. Full size, and he was small at under nine pounds, he was still ready to burst with joy. And then he died. Yesterday decided me."

"Yesterday decided you? What do you mean by that?"

"To get another cat?" Ash asked perplexedly.

"I saw him again."

"A horse?" Ash said, grasping.

"Who did you see?"

"That man, Eddy."

"Where did you see him?"

"I don't know much about horses, or Christmas in May, or much about," she hesitated, then said, "Derby. I don't want this terrible incident."

"The Derby?"

"The murder," Perch said quietly, sternly.

"Yes, that," the witness confirmed, "to define who I am, who I am going to be."

"I see."

"I hope so detective. I truly do hope so. I'm old enough to be who I want, and old enough to realize that I will lose that privilege soon enough."

"Like driving," Perch said simply.

"I will be a victim soon enough. But not today.

This thing," she began with the vaguest of euphemisms, "doesn't change anything. I won't let it. I got back on the horse.

My life is in the sun, in parks and gardens. That is where I pass my time. I think that whoever built Louisville felt the same."

"Like Cave Hill," Perch stated. Light and flowers. A recent windstorm had toppled century old trees and broken monuments, but life continued, even in a graveyard.

"Is that wrong?"

"It's your life. It's your decision."

"Despite this?"

She interpreted their silence as agreement.

"There are however other horses. It could have been me."

"We have other parks. How many parks do we have?" he directed the question to his colleague.

"Twelve," Ash replied confidently. "And those are just the large ones."

Perch did not correct the error.

"You may want to avoid Creason. Consider it an eclipse during your life in the sun."

"Why? Why that one park and not the rest of my world?"

"Prudence," Perch replied, annoyed that he had no better response.

"Is Eddy a suspect in this?"

The detectives hesitated too long.

"Or in something else?"

"We can't speak to other crimes," Ash said, knowing that it was wrong to have already done so.

"Can you speak enough to assure me that it is safe to walk through Creason park in broad daylight?"

"It should be," the young detective murmured, instantly regretting these words as well. He looked down.

"With this Eddy able to show up any minute?" she pursued.

Neither detective responded.

"Do you ride horses?"

"Not regularly," Percheron replied.

"I'm thinking of what he said a moment ago."

"About getting back in the saddle? That's just an expression."

"Even in Kentucky?"

Perch smiled in response.

"I don't ride myself," the woman said.

"What do you do?" Perch inquired. "Horses and riding are quite popular in..."

"And expensive. It wouldn't happen again. It never does, does it? Until it does strike again. I am rambling."

Emerald stood, shook their hands, and left.

Two days later, Emerald returned.

"I saw him outside the park."

"Who?"

"The murderer! Who else?"

Her excitement had no impact on Percheron.

"Where?" he asked, his politeness interpreted as boredom.

"I'm afraid detective," she added, turning to address the younger policeman.

He echoed his colleague's question.

"Where did you see the murderer?"

She did not answer either of them but continued with her own narrative.

"The first time, in the park, it was happenstance. I could have sat on a bench on the zoo side. There is a bench there near the top of the steep incline. The sun doesn't shine in my eyes on that side, not in the morning it doesn't. I wish that I had."

"That is the southern side," Percheron said, his voice factual. It was as much for his own benefit as for the witness.

"And then I came in the other day."

"I remember," Perch said, adding encouragement to his response.

"I thought that was it. Like a car, you see".

"What is like a car?"

"You buy a car, it doesn't matter which, and then... Well, I suppose if you bought some rare car, but who does? I don't."

"And?" the younger detective prompted. This witness was beginning to remind him of a non-favorite aunt.

"And then you see the same make and model, and color, always the same color, all over town."

"You saw his car? He has the same model car that you do? You didn't mention a car when we first spoke."

"No. Sorry detective. She turned to face the older of the two men.

"I'm not making myself clear. This is not about a car. I remember seeing him before."

"Where?"

"A better question is who?"

She was not to be distracted.

"That is the question I've been asking myself for hours."

"Was it in a grocery store? A laundromat. Hey, don't judge, we don't all live in Lake Forest. I still go to the laundromat."

"No, it wasn't one of those. I rent myself, and I use a laundromat. But, since all this, well the dirty clothes are just piling up. Maybe doing laundry would help. I don't know. I don't know where, you would think that I would remember, but I only had a glimpse of Eddy."

"Eddy?" Percheron asked.

"You remember seeing Eddy, and you think that he is the murderer, but you don't recall where you saw him? I find that difficult to...understand."

"It could have been here or there, I can't say for sure where because..."

"Because you only caught a glimpse?'

"Or because you are seeing him everywhere?" Perch added.

"That might be true. That would mean I'm imagining things. Either that or he is following me. Glimpses now and again, is he stealthy, or am I going crazy. Which is worse?"

Emerald frowned and continued.

"I just feel so strongly that I've seen him before, and since."

"Ok."

"Ok?"

"Yeah, you've seen him before, and since. I believe you."

The old woman and the young man visibly relaxed. A moment later the woman retensed and asked,

"And?"

"And, so what?"

The woman was taken aback.

"You've seen us again since the incident at Creason park. And your friends. You must have run into them before and since. What makes Eddy a murderer?"

"It stands to reason."

Perch said nothing.

"Doesn't it? Especially if..."

Perch remained silent, content to let the witness recount her theory at her own pace, in her own way. It was pure that way. Sometimes.

"I was the intended victim all along."

The young detective slammed back in the cheap chair, which squealed in protest.

"Thats possible, I suppose," Perch said.

"See, I'm right. What are you going to do about it? You will consider it?" Her voice pleaded for a whisper of support.

"Certainly," Perch offered soothingly.

"I will have my partner look into it personally."

"That is such a relief," she said, repeating aloud earlier thoughts.

"It would help nevertheless if you could remember one of the places that you recall, or think you might recall having seen Eddy. We need to have something to go on. We need to target our interviews."

The woman deflated.

"You do see our position." It was said almost as an instruction. The words were polite, but firm.

"If you could tell us the name of the laundromat you frequent?"

The woman was nonplussed.

"You make it sound so filthy, she said without a trace of irony. I don't frequent laundromats. Or bars."

"Not filthy, but dirty at times," Perch said, the words accompanied by a smile.

"It was the Carousel, on Whipps Mill, I think is the road."

"Perfect. I wonder why a man like Eddy would go to a laundromat."

"It's a lead," the other detective chirped in. "We'll catch him. He must have been trying to clean evidence."

"I used to be pleasant looking," she said unabashedly. She was still far beyond her modest description.

"I felt safe back then."

Percheron thought of the first witness. Like the passerby at the park, she too was alone, with no ties to Louisville. She had identified herself as Annie.

Crazy Annie she had added drily, a twinkle in her fatigued eyes.

"We are all crazy, don't you know? Crazy doesn't help identify us," she had said in rebuttal to the two detectives who stood in place of the countless, absent mockers.

Percheron had tried to locate her, first by himself, passing by the now usual, semipermanent neighborhoods for the increasingly stable homeless community. Like eggs left undisturbed they had hatched and staked a claim in the world.

As for Annie, she had disappeared. Whether she was dead, her corpse yet undiscovered, or she had been rescued by a concerned family member, or kidnapped by an equally anxious relative, or she had simply left town did not matter.

"We don't need her," Percheron said to Ash, realizing that the woman had been the object of such sentiment for many years. He sighed.

"Life is a tale," he added, not caring if Ash understood the allusion. A policeman would not need it explained.

"She provided us a clue. Her testimony wouldn't help."

Ash nodded.

"It might hurt the case. She isn't really an asset. If..."

Percheron gave Ash his full attention.

"If it comes to that, we just..."

"Tell the truth?" Percheron suggested.

"Yeah, we tell the truth. The witness disappeared."

## CHAPTER FIFTEEN

He had not been in the Tiki Bar for a very long time. It offered a faint, moldy smell, combined with a slickness on everything inside: the bar surface, the menu, even the roughhewn beams were more than halfway through their conversion. It was an ancient, no longer fashionable recipe of spilled alcohol and tobacco smoke residue, dried to a varnish like texture.

A six foot long, oversized Louisville slugger was mounted horizontally over the bar. It reminded him of the broom that he had seen placed over the doorway of a restaurant in rural France. Both sections of wood served the same purpose, to amuse the innocent and to warn others. In this case, the baseball bat was tipped in red wax, like the well-known bourbon, mixing two local icons.

The odor of the restaurant was like the perfume section of department stores that Eddy used to visit for gifts, back when...but that was back then. It was the sort of smell that one gets used to, but doing so demanded more time than Eddy was willing to invest. Behind the bar, in front of the stove, the cook was occupied with several orders. It was old, a bit grimy, but it was authentic. And that was important, Eddy thought pleasantly, an emotion that he was finding more and more difficult to conjure. Pleasure was fading more quickly, and more permanently, than the memory of scent loving past loves.

In a few weeks, their attention would turn to the NFL. Brutal crime declined during football season. Vicarious violence was effective as how many officers? Maybe they should extend the season. A few years of peace would be welcome. He glanced at the man in the kitchen, all dressed in black, as seemed to be the required uniform for all servers and cooks. Tales was not a foodie place. It had been a long time since Eddy had set foot in the place, a longtime neighborhood, opened before he had been born.

He ordered a beer and noticed dispassionately the arthritic fingers of the bartender as she placed the drink on the bar before him. The establishment was decorated like some Caribbean watering hole. The bar itself was called the Tiki, and palm trees decorated the menu. It was from a time when cruises were only experienced only through television.

Tales survived, supported by locals and their children. It offered an escape, a tropical image, and he thought that it was not all that different than the games he created and marketed. His was the more addictive he thought, and more profitable. Still, it was a nice change, he thought, as he ordered a second beer and studied the menu.

The bar was crowded, with men and women seated on bar stools like swaying sea urchins awaiting fertilization float by.

His seatmate had stopped at Kroger for a quart of milk, but finding the parking full, had instead stopped in for a pint of beer. The man, Craig something, went on and on about some old car that he was restoring. It was an anniversary gift by the husband for the wife. Or was it the other way round? Eddy didn't much listen and had commented that it was more romantic than a replacement hip, or a newer, trophy spouse. His listening had become halfhearted, even to his own words, as if nothing novel would be spoken ever again. The sole exception was when he was in hunting mode and not sated as he was now.

Craig finished his draft and left.

"Did lions feel this way?" Eddy wondered idly and pictured himself as an alpha predator. Maybe he should let his hair grow. He scanned around half seriously. The best victims advertised themselves. They approached him in response to a few words of encouragement on his part. He uttered a few bleeps disguised as compliments, and they came like coyotes to a call carrying hunter. He had merely to exhale a few meaningless phrases and they stood before him or sat beside him unhesitatingly. He would pass tonight, for no reason other than he was beginning to tire of the game.

God himself could not stick permanently to one role. Murder, other than random slaying, was too much like work. Hell, it was work. There were no multiple plays for a dollar if he committed an error, no do-overs, no respawning. This was real life and yet it was sinking into boredom. Was this yet another video game knockoff? They was all variations of shoot and kill, including the silly version that was streaming from the oversized screen at that very moment. Grown men in shorts; it was all so pathetic. More and more broadcasters were women, it was like conscientious sisters doing their utmost to bring interest to their sibling ridiculous antics. Had the league hired them to reverse declining ratings? He didn't care; it was all background noise and flashing lights.

A woman took Craig's empty seat and began her stalk.

He glanced and her and then away. She was off limits, like the large yellow diamond he had seen at Galleries Lafayette in Paris. The price was marked, here it might just have well as been. The woman was neither yellow nor chocolate, but his brief observation had brought the image of the French jewel to mind

His ears were sore. How could anyone talk so much and say so little?

He said nothing to encourage the stranger, and she soon left. He should have chosen an end seat to minimize human contact.

A shower would improve his mood. It was a crime that the inventor of such a stress relieving pleasure had not received the Nobel peace prize, or statues erected in his honor. Aside from a few disparaging movie scenes, nothing malevolent occurred within the confines of the gushing water. It was a daily baptism in his private, inhouse chapel.

"It makes you angry?" He heard one woman ask another. They were seated at a neighboring table.

"Of course it makes me angry."

"It's unhealthy, the first admonished. I read it recently."

"You can find someone to tell you anything you want. That isn't what I need."

Eddy regarded the women for a polite moment, then turned away before he ventured into intrusion. He could not identify either of them, but they looked familiar, in the troubling way that too many people, not just women, looked increasingly familiar. Faces were beginning to repeat. Had he filled his brain with all variations of the human face? It was making him angry, the state the two women were debating, in a manner that was itself maddening. Was this his future, a sepia toned world that would deteriorate into fewer and fewer images, were eventually he would be staring at nothing but himself in a mirror?

He stretched his shoulders, sitting more erect. He closed his eyes for a moment then reopened them and glanced quickly around at the entire restaurant.

Each face was as should be, unique. That was reality. Each self-contained a book, a handful of interest, more worth a second glance or a brief conversation. They could be means to an ending, while an internal gnawing somewhere inside his own being suggested that this ending might itself possess no meaning.

He was as drunk as God behaves. But for neither was the source alcohol.

He ignored the police. His experiment would succeed or fail despite their best efforts. Or his own, he added ruefully. Experiments typically have a control. What was his? Other killers? He sighed. That item was well covered.

Should he have hidden other bodies? Had God outsourced omniscience to the google headline news? It seemed that way. The press, however, had not uttered a word about a serial murderer. If they had any hint of such a publicity windfall, they would have screamed it by now. The local town criers would have been unstoppable.

Screw them too, Eddy thought. This was his show, and they would remain oblivious members of the audience. One critic alone mattered.

Sleep and alcohol to induce sleep were the only relief, each slumber delicious with the possibility that it would be permanent. Not death, but eternal sleep, waking in a quieter, calmer word not impossible, but not expected either. Each sleep regretted the following morning as he woke to sound.

Eddy recognized the couple that had taken seats in the restaurant. They were regulars at a local sports bar. According to one of the female servers there, they led a certain lifestyle. Swingers he translated. Upon hearing that, they became protected, exempt from his plan. Any smiting would need to be done by another, less discerning agent.

In the past, he would have been intrigued, taken by the woman's overall appearance, but as of now he was in search of more pristine game.

A young woman sat next to Eddy and ordered a coke, which she had no time to drink as she was glued to her phone.

She wanted to be pregnant forever. It was the only project she had, and she wanted to extend it indefinitely. Once delivered, the new life would signify the end of hers.

Her laugh was a passable copy of her cell phone's odd ringtone. Was she talking to someone else, or to someone at the bar? Phones were more annoying than pets in a restaurant.

He tossed a look at the woman. She was off limits with her pregnatic immunity. His gaze moved on, then paused. He considered a moment then slowly swiveled his head to regard her more carefully. His eyes directly on her, he studied the woman as if he had never seen one.

He would kill her, he thought as dispassionately as he would select a lobster from its coffin shaped tank.

This must be considered distasteful by the deity of any religion. Not halal, not kosher, simply not.

She was perfect.

He would be faithfully evil. Or was it faithlessly, he wondered, only for a moment.

Eddy ordered an Arnold Palmer. He sipped the beverage, savoring each taste as a drop of murderous intent. He sat back and considered his options, confident that the lemony sugar would spur thoughts while the special component in the tea would moderate his enthusiasm. It might also unlock regrets over this game. Soon it worked its natural magic and he scribbled the essence of the idea presented. He would not trust his memory. Not here, seated at a bar.

He was unwilling to wait thirty, forty, fifty years and let the mystery resolve itself. By then he would be too weak, too consumed by constant argument. The time was now.

The camera flash from a nearby iPhone reminded him that God might not be ever present, but Apple sure was.

Was he crazy? He wondered. If so, it wasn't as bad as doctors claimed. But then they diagnosed, prescribed, and cashed the treatment check.

"No, I'm tired, nothing more. I'm not crazy, I am not intoxicated. None of the above. Not yet. Tired, and semi everything else, conditions which pass for normal in this society. So many humans trying to outweird the latest fool on the tube."

He was glad when the pre-mother left. Eddy ordered a beer and struck up a conversation with the man to his left. The man ported a sweater embossed with Kauai and claimed in a cancer-tinged whisper that he would return there soon.

"I write eulogies for a living," he said without irony.

"Eulogies? For dead people?"

The man had been in enough bars in his life to have learned to overlook stupid questions.

"Death doesn't equal dates," he responded.

"What?"

"It's more than dates. Never a complaint from them. Not from their family who write the checks. Folks pay from grief or remorse. Grief pays double usually. No one is that remorseful.

"Remorse is good for the soul," the cliché escaped from Eddy's lips.

"I know you ain't a cop or a lawyer. Why talk like one? You must be running for office. You don't have a chance."

"Why not?"

His seat mate reappraised him like a car he might be interested in. He frowned and shook his head as double strikes, then took a long drink of beer that completed the out.

"You ain't got the right look."

"What is the right look?"

"I can't say for sure, but you ain't got it."

"Thanks for the vote of confidence."

The comment passed unremarked.

"I'm considering," then bragged, "I'm developing a new video game."

His companion perked up.

"I knew you was a nerd."

Eddy ignored the expression that was equal parts compliment and insult.

"Like GTA?" the man pursued.

"Better."

What could be better than GTA? Maybe BB," he suggested, the acronym lost on Eddy.

"You will have to wait and see," Eddy responded, then added, as payback for nerd, "and experience it."

The man was quiet, reflecting on God knew what he envisioned as a better GTA.

Eddy suddenly felt powerfully evil, seeing his scant words erupt as a full-blown temptation in this stranger's mind. Eddy downed his beer to freeze the moment into permanence in his own memory.

"Cops and robbers isn't really a game," the man said.

"We know. That's why we play it," Eddy said conspiratorially. "We all know it isn't a game," he repeated the stranger's statement confidently.

"How could you improve GTA?"

"Believe me my friend, there are ways."


Eddy looked at the note that lay on the passenger seat of his car. The note was not his

It was not directed to him. He was not even sure that it was a note.

Whatever it was, it had been torn from some book or magazine. Only young and old people touched paper these days, he mused. And a few college students he added. Were they young? Not most of them. They not only acted old, they were old. Wonderful customers they had been for him, as they gleefully accepted his imagination as their own.

The note sat there patiently, content to outwait Eddy.

Eddy leaned to retrieve it, to see if the reverse had equally mysterious. He stopped himself. Reaching into the rear, he pulled a Kleenex from the box that sat on the seat, a necessity during the never-ending allergy season. Using the tissue as a makeshift glove, he lifted the sheet for closer inspection.

A few small, oblong shapes nestled in the upper right-hand corner, like a rust-colored Rorschach exam. He failed to see any meaning in the blobs. You suck as a prophet he thought.

The reverse was totally empty, equally devoid of insight. He was perplexed, a bit bemused. Eddy returned the paper to its original orientation. The writing, if that was what it was, remained as unfathomable as the blank side.

Was it Greek? Dots underneath various characters reminded him of the Braille he had seen on elevator control panels, but that made no sense here, for the paper was printed, not embossed. An instruction guide for teachers of Braille. The school and printing house for the blind was here in Louisville, Eddy recalled.

He shrugged. The day was advancing, leaving him behind. He snapped a quick photo of the front sheet, then crumpled it into a tissue wrapped ball and relegated it to future disposal. He frowned at the unassuming enigma, annoyed at its presence.

Once home, Eddy brought up Youtube to rewatch one brief scene in Zero Dark Thirty. The actress said, "He's there. And you are going to kill him for me." It was the most erotic of lines, it was beyond hot, it was incandescent.

# CHAPTER SIXTEEN

Eddy took stock of his progress. He had done it all. Cosplay, larp, rugby, online games without count, old time videos, an excessive number of tours in what was now a call to monotony.

Even a stint with an older cousin and his dungeons and dragons cohort. They never ventured beyond that gateway drug. IRL, or in the alleged matrix, it had all been sampled and resampled, in what he now saw was a decade long expedition in the land of wasted time.

Soon, he would be categorized as one with no chance of respawning.

This was a bust, no one was showing. He had arrived early that first day. He had always been a good student.

But this was a bust, a waste of time. Another waste of time. But not much. He had avoided being sucked into another vacuum that dissipated real life.

So much for being a conscientious student. As a teacher he would have... he thought, then stopped and said aloud, "I will be the teacher. I am the teacher. Traquant Dieu," he liked the title, the concept somewhat religious in nature, he had to admit that it was a bit vague on details. So much the better, now that this was his game. Or was it? He had the sense that the original player was still online, if only part time. Or was it himself, drunk at night? Was he playing against himself. This was fun and annoying, a game pulsating so quickly between pleasure and pain that is was dizzying. My game, he had suddenly and totally decided, he remembered. My rules. He would create and master his own game.

"But how?" he questioned himself.

He thought, looking around, hoping for a place where he could sit and think.

He'd drunk too much that night, he had a dim recollection of a vow he'd made to himself, of which he could not recall the details.

Eddy had recognized Percheron at Paristown, the day of the message.

Someone had started his game. Or was it yourself, an inner voice interrogated.

"That's crazy," he replied aloud. Still, he thought, having an inner voice to which one answered aloud in public was what, other than crazy?

Should he call the police? He recalled having seen Percheron at Paristown, the day that he had posted the flyer. That was real, wasn't it?

The day I saw the flyer.

"The one you posted," his inquisitor accused.

"That was not me," he shouted, drawing stares from the few who were not themselves lost in their electronic devices. One of them hurriedly packed up and left, Eddy noticed.

"Maybe the police were already tracking the killer."

"They've been watching you Eddy," taunted the voice.

Eddy too, hurriedly packed and left. He could scream at his tormentor from the solitude of his car.

But if he was crazy, or worse, they would arrest him. He'd be released if insane, there was irony buried somewhere in that process. He'd be homeless, not right away, but it would be the inevitable result.

Or they would arrest him. For what? For having taken a stranger's idea for a game and extended it to death? Thoughts weren't illegal. He asked himself without his accuser needing to speak.

"What if you've done more?"

Eddy attempted to recall what he had in fact done, the day and night of the first two murders. For one he had no alibi than he was blacked out drunk. As for the second, he was clearly innocent. His moments were perfectly accounted for.

"Too perfectly," his inner voice suggested.

"Your memory is electrical impulses that trigger chemical reactions. And you trust that?"

Eddy laughed. Only he would have a degreed second personality.

But the mocker had a point. His memory differed little from an online video game, one with no backup. He himself had no corroboration from his friends. He had spent the day exercising and the evening reading. Leftovers for dinner. Uneventful.

His accuser had no rebuttal, but Eddy recognized that he needed none. Eddy breathed a sigh of relief but understood that his alibi was pitiful and so innocent as to appear implausible.

He frowned. If he questioned his own whereabouts, so would the police. As would his friends and family.

He asked himself again if he should alert the police?

He could join in the game, cosplay for a while, an apprenticeship, or both?

Cosplay.

What was the game? He remembered now, the goal returning to his mind as rapidly as if it were a freshly created memory.

To stalk God. To bring Him to bay. Traquant Dieu, he repeated. And where more appropriate for the climax than at the culprit's residence?

He looked at his notebook, one page with a few words scribbled, several scratched out.

Baptist, Catholic, Jew, Muslim.

Eddy was content with his list, it was short, manageable, he wasn't Noah, laughing at his own wit.

He rose, went to his bedroom, stripped, showered, redressed and went to see God, at one of his many mansions.

# CHAPTER SEVENTEEN

The man, not much older than himself Percheron observed, was chewing the meat from the rib slowly, tilting his head noticeably to the left, favoring the teeth on that side. The image reminded him of a chocolate Labrador that his family had when he was a child. The memory had lain dormant in his brain for how long, only to be raised from its gray resting place for this moment.

Slow and contented, this stranger and the long dead household pet. One gone, the other and he himself to trail the hound at some time in the not-so-distant future.

"Not today," Percheron said aloud. He had work to perform, his own days of hunting not yet a fading memory.

His retired friends, such as they were, would have mocked his maudlin attitude. If they had been aware of its severity, they would have suggested counseling. As to themselves, retirement was a long delayed, well deserved lifelong summer vacation, and not a brief stay in an airport lounge before final departure. Their golden years were not perceived as the waiting room to oblivion; a jail bereft of cells.

"Not today," Percheron repeated, for he had a case to solve. It was a terrible crime, but, in his eyes, beautiful beyond measure. It was life and youth itself.

Percheron glanced again at the diner, just in time to see him belch, slowly and contentedly. For a man to whom few moments remained, he was obstinate in savoring each one. Joie de vivre, Percheron concluded. The detective rose slowly, adopting the diner's attitude toward time, then regained his normal composure and hurried toward the exit. The door closed behind Percheron, as the diner, emulating the long dead lab, passed gas.

# CHAPTER EIGHTEEN

"These crimes are odd."

The other detective looked at Perch expectantly.

"They are odd in that none of the victims had any enemies."

"Apparently not, but obviously they did," the younger man ventured.

"Attendance at these funerals is huge. None were celebrities, but all were popular within their communities."

Percheron recited from a list.

"Business, church, arts, charities. Et cetera, et cetera."

"It's almost like the same person is being murdered. That is super weird."

"Is that the connection?"

"Who knows?"

"We will."

He looked again at the photos, and the younger man wondered if Percheron expected one of them to speak.

"Maybe it is. Or maybe there are a lot of good people in Louisville. That's just as likely. Maybe."

"Still, it's odd. The crime has attributes of both being personal and detached."

"How can that be? It can't be both."

"Can't it?" Percheron said with a smile.

"It strikes me that they are in fact both. Killed, and obscured. Like a predator. Whoever this person is, he does not want the bodies to be found right away, but they aren't well and truly hidden.

"The victim in the park?"

"I'm not sure. Maybe he was in more of a hurry. He doesn't pose or display them in some bizarre manner. He kills, covers the body, or not, and moves on like..."

"Like a fox in a hen house, or a pack of wolves?"

"I was thinking more like a, oh not a soldier, but someone on a mission."

"So, he wants the bodies found, but not immediately. He has more important tasks than murder?"

"That is what the evidence tells me."

The younger man wished that he had recorded Percheron's last sentence, it was so Perch. Instead, he simply noted it in his notebook, with a star beside it.

"I don't believe that he has a preference one way or the other as to what anyone else thinks or does. He kills and moves on.

"Why would he do that?"

"You need a body to collect on life insurance without having to wait months if not years. You need a body found to make the news."

"He could be passing through and doesn't worry about the debris left behind. Like a hotel room. Or a homeless person."

"You need a body to have a funeral," the young detective said, then immediately felt foolish when Percheron stopped his pacing and stared at him.

"What did you say?"

"Nothing. Sorry."

"Please, repeat it."

"You need to have a body to have a funeral."

"That is genius, Ash."

Ash blushed at the insult, then blushed more deeply when he realized that the words were a compliment.

"We need videos from the funerals, anyone out of place or not recognized by the family. Who knows each and every attendee? The press was there, as were emotional sponges and assorted kooks. See what you can do."

But Perch sensed that the actual killer had other plans for that date and time.

They spent the next day reviewing footage and photographs. Mourners, a few were hunched and moved from car to open grave and back with a crablike walk, the return shuffle more rapid, the detectives noticed. The elderly ported grey hair, sensible shoes, but none of the excess pounds worn by the younger attendees.

They ran it through some facial recognition software, and it identified a few more matches than they had found themselves.

The following day they discussed their findings.

"He isn't there."

"How can we determine that? They are so well attended."

"A few people have been at more than one, no one has been to three or more except."

"Except who?"

"Us."

The pronoun hung in the air.

"A few of officers in plain clothes, you and me, in short a handful of us."

"You can't..."

"I have to Ash."

Percheron gathered his thoughts.

"To be honest, I don't consider this a possibility, but you understand. Everyone involved in this case, police I mean, are considering all possibilities, including this one. Us."

# CHAPTER NINETEEN

Percheron and Eddy both lived in Lake Forest. The detective resided in one of the first houses built in the now sprawling subdivision, back when he believed that a normal future awaited him. Eddy resided in the estate section, over a mile away, in a huge home he had purchased when he knew the opposite.

Both residences were well maintained, the landscaping adequate for their respective class, both equally empty of the possessions and family that filled the homes of their neighbors.

Eddy swiveled in his chair, breaking the mental connection with the internet. Sometimes it was worse than sacrificing a day to a marathon of football. Watching grown men chase one another was very strange when one considered it.

He needed a break from chasing God. Women were easier to catch.

He showered, shaved, and dressed in upscale casual, deciding at the last moment to wear a silk sports coat.

He decided on a place in Nulu, a new restaurant in an old part of town, freshly painted.

Eddy sat in the bar, a popular chapel for fervent believers in alcohol. It was a wonderfully typical bar, the last public refuge for liberty, where one was free to carry one's freedoms carefully concealed deadly weapons included, an alcohol spiced stage of a life that seemed to be rapidly fading to sepia.

A man at the corner of the bar was speaking loudly, his voice was reedy, like a video of bygone politicians from a forgotten era. In addition to his voice, the man was noticeable by the frequent absences from his companion, likely his wife. Given the man's age, Eddy suspected prostate issues, but he drank little, his preferred cancer being the pulmonary variety, and his numerous sojourns outside offered proof of his devotion to acquiring the illness, as well at the limits of freedom in the tobacco free saloon.

The man's voice was remarkable. Its tone was memorable, not unpleasant. Eddy had assumed at first that it was an impromptu performance, an impression of some unheard-of celebrity. He soon realized its authenticity as the owner's voice continued to speak of mundane manners, its peculiar frequency piercing the drone of the other conversations in the bar.

He was short, white bearded, with an equally silver trimmed mustache. His hair was similarly colored, worn swept back, and slightly damp. His face was lined with a perfect scale of respectable wrinkles. Eddy was grateful for the diversion and was disappointed when the voice stopped.

Eddy did not turn his head despite having heard the drop in volume of the surrounding conversations. It was a spontaneous, shared hesitation, a pause that followed the arrival of someone, its amplitude evidence that it was a woman, its length proof of her attractiveness.

He did not turn to follow the bargoers' gaze. He was beyond that today. She was their distraction, not his.

Vastly more important matters lay before him: life, death. And beyond. What was she, compared to the alleged master of the universe?

He faced straight ahead, not deigning to notice her, emulating self-consciously the deity whose existence he doubted.

His studied indifference collapsed as the object of the bar's attention stopped and tapped him on the shoulder. It was more of a poke, he decided, as he turned to face the woman.

"Are you lost? Or are you simply ignoring me?"

"Surely the former, Kimberly," he said, her name coming to him in time for it to be appended seamlessly to his response.

"You are not a member of the ignorable class."

Kimberly Fredricks appraised him doubtfully, then concluded that it didn't matter if he was truthful or not.

"Good," she said, one word that could have easily been translated as 'agreed'.

"Have you been stood up, again?" Kimberly asked, but she did not wait for a reply.

"Are you still going?"

"To Paris?"

"Yes, like you said on our...the other day."

Date was a four-letter word for women of Kimberly's age.

"Yes, soon."

The woman nodded. Eddy was not sure what that meant, so he remained silent.

"I would ask you what you do but."

"But what?"

"You would be obligated to ask me what I do and my answer would not be as good as yours."

"I don't believe in obligations. Is that better?"

The man next to them moved down one stool and Kimberly filled the empty seat.

"Thanks," she said to the stranger. To Eddy, she replied, "I doubt it."

"I used to do what others asked me, told me really."

Kimberly nodded.

"And then I did what I wanted. I still do."

Kimberly opened her mouth to speak but pursed them closed as Eddy continued.

"But that is not enough."

"What else is there?"

"What else indeed?"

"I imagine doing what you want covers a great deal. Including buying me a drink before you take me dancing.

"I imagine more."

"Like what for instance?"

He thought for a long moment.

Kimberly spoke. She was used to filling in the holes in conversations that men invariably dug.

"There is archeology."

Eddy laughed.

"Where did that come from?"

Her comment had had the intended effect.

Men are so predictable she thought.

"When men are really bored with life, and I mean really bored, they start digging in someone else's past, because the life of a long dead stranger must have been exciting.  History is the male version of a soap opera.  Neither is real."

Kimberly took a sip of her cocktail then leaned close to Eddy and whispered, as if confiding a terrible secret, "I can't believe that you took me to a church that first day."

She leaned back and asked in a normal voice, "You can dance, can't you?"

"You are wrong about me Kim.  Not that, yes, I can dance.  History is dead to me."

"And the present."

"On life support."

"And the future?"

"Bleak."

"Well at least you're not a pessimist.  Even though your friend hasn't shown for Happy Hour."

"Who?"

"Your mysterious, absent acquaintance.  You could interpret his ghosting you as a sign."

She took his silence as curiosity but elected to proceed cautiously.

"If I'm prying Eddy, well, go with it.  As a man you need to be pried occasionally."

"Paris.  Soon"

"Most men say things like that."

"I'm not most men."

"They say that too."

Kimberly thought, wondering what to say. This man was different, younger than her usual fare. But it was more to it. Younger, yes, but more serious, less attentive. She couldn't describe it perfectly. He wasn't jaded as an older man might be. He was confident but not overtly ambitious. It wasn't as if he wasn't assured of where he was going but more that he knew where he was, was content with the situation and was waiting, with growing impatience for the rest of the world to catch up. It was an attitude unlike that of anyone else she knew. It was alluring because it was simultaneously peaceful and frightening. He was almost still a boy. He was certainly attracted to sci-fi and religion. If she kept him for long he would need to be housebroken if he didn't soon outgrow them. She had nothing against fantasy, but it had to be fun.

All those thoughts raced through her mind. When she opened her mouth to speak, she had no words prepared. Kimberly found that irksome.

Eddy filled the void.

"I am one man."

He could sense the gaze of the other patrons upon them, then heard the murmuring inside the bar increase as they resumed their conversations, "Reedy" included.

Eddy tolerated Kimberly. She existed for him not as a diversion but as an unwitting accomplice. In his solitary game, he had no need of a sounding board. She likely considered him dangerous, probably criminal. He was her final bad boy, he imagined her telling herself, and that she had unknowingly saved the worst for last.

120

His not being her type was her type, Kimberly had in fact convinced herself. Playing with fire was addictive. She had always been weak when it came to the strength of...hell, any strength. Her internal burn scars doubled as fondly remembered trophies.

Eddy appraised her again. She acquiesced too easily. Could she be a master player in this game which he know believed to be solitary, his alone. Was her predilection for darkness feigned? Could it be that her blasé acceptance to evil was itself a disguise for her own level of depravity that surpassed his own. Was he dreaming, or living a nightmare that was extending its duration each passing day?

This game, it was good. It not only mirrored reality, but was on the verge of displacing it. It was another unexpected level in this non-repetitive game. The number of new entrants was unlimited, there was no ante. His prior experience as a gamer was devalued to near zero. He had grasped this game from the original, seeming absent designer, at Portland cemetery. He had torn it away as if it were a purse to be snatched. There he had crowned himself conqueror and director, but now here, with potential players all about, including this beautiful woman sitting beside him, he considered that he might be no more than an extra.

Was he insane? How much damage, real or only fantasy, would he cause before the game ended? He was not one to surrender or to admit defeat. This self-administered slap to his arrogance was welcome. Let the game recommence.

Eddy's mind returned to Nulu.

"In twelve days. Freedom?" Eddy asked her, not expecting an answer.

"Adventure?" he prompted.

"Maybe. Why not? Are you alone?"

"What?"

"Are you with someone tonight?"

"Yes. No. Sorry. Yes, I'm alone tonight."

"We could be alone together."

"No, not tonight. I'm sorry, Kimberly. I meant in twelve days. In Paris. I'm leaving."

"Leaving?"

"Leaving. I don't remember if I mentioned it on our first date."

Kimberly frowned.

"My memory is not as good as it once was. I remember..."

"I remember that you didn't say that I was beautiful."

Eddy smiled and made a motion with his hand to the mirror behind the bar.

"The glass offers constant compliments of the obvious Kimberly."

Kimberly sighed mentally.

"It would be an adventure as you said."

"Think it over."

"I will."

"I'd like to talk more about this, but I have an appointment in a few minutes."

Kimberly smiled to mask her disappointment.

"A rendezvous with your mysterious friend from the other day?"

Eddy returned her smile with his own.

"You may just be right. I will let you know. We will dance another time, I promise. He stood and left; the bar not expectantly silent for him as he exited.

It was raining on the short walk across the parking lot. It was a light brief shower, one that served only to shake and awaken from their slumber the bacteria that inhabited the seasonal dust. Their exhaled exclamation at having been disturbed brought to the Eddy's nostrils the unmistakable scent of summer.

# CHAPTER TWENTY

Annie's wisdom was the sort that accrues through survival. She possessed sufficient experience to recognize her chronic ability to make poor decisions, and wise enough to be resigned to their consequences.

She had pushed her cart of worldly goods to the Hyatt Regency on Fourth Street and entered its Starbucks. Content to leave the bulk of her possessions on the curb outside. She could observe it through one of the large windows, aware that she could do nothing to prevent its theft. The woman took with her only a large duffel bag, plastic, torn but mostly waterproof. It contained what an average observer would classify as paltry, one half step above rubbish. To her it was the holy of holies, relics of what had once been her life, combined with the necessities to maintain what now passed for existence.

Annie regarded her belongings. They would not have filled a cardboard box from a liquor store. Her world consisted of memories and a few plans. That was what you needed, all that was really yours. Memories, nothing except memories. Those eventually evaporated, she suspected. But which ones? The most painful, Annie hoped. Still, she had plenty, more than enough to fill a warehouse of cardboard boxes. And a few plans. She laughed unconsciously, confirming for her fellow café customers their opinion of the homeless woman whom they wished was not there, not even as a memory.

She ordered the most ornate of coffee drinks and settled in. Maybe it was time to leave this town. North? South? She could afford a bus ticket. She had given the cops enough information, all that she had. Or nearly so. Fair was fair was a lesson she had mislearned.

"When it comes to what they think is important, I'm thirty seconds behind," Annie spoke aloud, aware that no one understood her words as they avoided hearing them. "Half a minute isn't bad," she said, remembering her long ago. "When it comes to what matters to me, I am far ahead." Annie's claim went unnoticed.

She studied the card that the older detective had given to her in case she remembered anything else. The small piece of stiff paper was worth its weight in gold, for a while. It was good throughout the country, an unexpired stay of out jail card. She placed it carefully in the faithful pouch that lay between her breasts. Maybe she would stay a few more days.

# CHAPTER TWENTY-ONE

"There was something special about Mark. He was a renaissance man, a term I would not have known at that time we first met.

Mark was a good student, a good basketball player, he studied Latin instead of French. He was friendly yet mature beyond his years, another phrase that I came to appreciate later.

To those adults of those past years who did appreciate that compliment, mature beyond his years, they tended to characterize him as "that smart ass kid."

You have to be smart to be a wise ass.

As a mentioned we met in high school, where children who have committed no crime are thrown together to serve four years."

Perch smiled at the comment, spoken by one stranger about his friend, another stranger to the detective.

"Mark and myself stayed in touch over the decades since, whether via phone, my annual visits back here, or Mark's trips to see me in whatever city was home. During his visits, he would quickly discover places unknown to me, and just as rapidly meet and make new friends.

Truth be told, many of them were attractive women.  I remember once...but no, I will leave that anecdote for another day.

I say that Mark was a renaissance man, which the uninformed envision as a ne'er do well with a bit of education and a clean suit.  A renaissance man, or woman, does indeed possess those two items, but above all, such a person, must, as was my dear, late friend, be practical.

Practical in understanding that our years are limited, that you can't have it all in the time allotted, that even if you could, you would need to return all the toys to the closet when recess is called over.

I was awakened at 3:18, in the morning, shortly after Mark died.  It was not by his sister Michelle, who would call me a few hours later.  It was by my late friend, who, I believe, after he regreeted relatives who had gone on before, and likely several dogs, took a moment to let me know that he had arrived safely on his final voyage.

He leaves behind many friends and family who will cherish memories of Mark until we meet again.

I miss him.

Mark understood that the true crime in life is to not enjoy what you have; friends, family, abandoned dogs rescued.

I miss him," the stranger repeated.

As he exited the church, Percheron glanced at his watch. The service had been brief for a life that had been long.

"Where were you?"

Perch raised an eyebrow before responding, "I went to a funeral."

The assistant raised both of his eyebrows in return.

"Another serial killing?"

"I doubt it."

"A friend "

"No, a complete stranger. My loss."

Perch noticed the expression on his assistant's face. It was curiosity overlaid by hesitancy.

"I don't know everyone and those I don't aren't always murdered. Listening to the eulogy of a good person, one not murdered that it, makes me feel better."

"It renews your faith in mankind?" Ash ventured. Perch looked steadily at the other detective. They both knew the answer to stupid questions. It was an old joke, a traditional method of terminating one conversation and transitioning to another.

The two detectives had each passed Redemption years ago in their respective careers, and there was no return.

# CHAPTER TWENTY-TWO

It was an odd choice; one she chose only because it felt safe from the interest of others. Men there were either in the company of their long-term wives, or dead, represented by their short term widows. Her own parents had loved the place. They had adored the 70's dinner club vibe and subdued décor. Unlike the restaurant, both of her parents were now gone.

As for herself, Kim had too many men in the past, and one or two more than ideal in the present. She would need to choose, soon. Kim had chosen poorly in the past as her father had scolded her during his numerous judgements.

So had her mother, she had wished to retort at each sentencing, but in balancing cruelty and kindness she had landed on the weaker, softer side.

Kim ordered a Lemon vodka martini in memory of her mother and smiled.

Her expression froze when she thought of Eddy. The man puzzled her. Their first 'date', with the stopover at a church, had been a shock. It was so unexpected and yet so familiar. Being driven to a house of worship by a man brought back memories of the distant past. At the time, she had nearly exited the vehicle and called for an Uber. Kimberly had no desire to have a religious man in her life again. As it turned out, she was pleased that she had remained seated. Eddy's subsequent actions had allayed her fears. They were more alike than... than what she could not answer.

She looked around the restaurant, as if seeing it for the first time. She should bring him here, Kimberly said to herself. If he hates it, perfect. And if he liked it? That would not be a catastrophe either, she decided. Her smile returned, just in time as the chilled drink landed in front of her.

Customers arrived and in departed in solos and pairs, larger groups rare. The bar was a destination without the need to pass through the unpleasantries of air travel. Flight had become difficult, made deliberately so, and annoying. Just when you can, you can't. She had left her cell phone at home, turned off, wrapped in plastic wrap, and then again in aluminum foil and placed in the refrigerator.

Maybe she could think without interruption. She really should just dispose of the tracking device. But she was addicted, as was everyone else.

Just when you can, you can't. The words echoed in her head like the lyrics of a nearly forgotten pop tune. Cyndi Lauper, she envisioned, would smash it. Instead, the phrase smashed her. She was on the cusp of age that would signify for her, just when you can, you can't.

She thought again of her dad. He could not manage without his church. Men cannot manage alone. Nor women. Just when you can, you can't.

# CHAPTER TWENTY-THREE

Eddy woke earlier and earlier despite drinking more and more. He was hesitant to expose himself to any news. This game was coming to occupy too much of his time. Time he had only recently found to be vacant and passing glacially.

And the booze, it was performance diminishing, in all of the ways that mattered. He was in need of performance, if not soberness or politeness, or polite soberness. He wanted to sleep, but was that too a thief of himself, another villain?

A villain. His online games had been overfilled with them, a near endless mass of them to overcome. Ironically in his real life adventure they could be ignored. Or disposed of if one persisted in being disruptive.

Villains don't kill one another he lied to himself.

He might waste a murder in killing someone who merited a nasty Christmas gift. That would not do at all.

Christmas, that was a happy time? So happy that they had cloned it into July. Xmas 2.0.

Was that the supreme taste of madness, he wondered. Insanity in July, as bizarre as Santa in the same pagan month. The idea had arrived uninvited. The flimsiest reason sufficed for a get together.

Christmas in July provided the template for other knockoff parties.

He would cruise Lake Forest and follow guests into whatever event they were attending, trusting his new found luck. How hilarious, he thought. If Chaos was the answer. He considered bringing a date, but that was beyond foolish. It was simpler to arrive and depart alone, as in life. He had driven into the non-estate section of the affluent neighborhood taking with him two gifts, one for a child, and a bottle of nonalcoholic cider. Seeing no balloons or children among other arrivals, he tossed the gaily decorated box on the rear seat, grabbed the cider, exited the vehicle, stepped rapidly to merge with a small group, and entered the spacious house with them.

It was Christmas morning inside, games, Santas in abundance, all props correct in their secularity. Some of the women wore sleeveless Christmas attire, a few wore festive hats. Only one attendee had arrived costumed as an uninvited guest.

The sound of the locomotive enveloped the spectators. The smell of wood smoke wafted by. Their senses confused by the recessed loudspeakers and scented candles, their eyes surrendered and magnified the size of the model train as it made its way around the large track that had been constructed in the basement. Eddy's attention was distracted from his prospective prey.

The scene in the basement was peaceful, nearly bucolic. It was summer in some small rural town, where the model businesses had no iron bars and the miniature public places were free of graffiti. It was a perfect summer day in the land of the tiny train. Like here, today, Eddy mused.

The sole concession to the boy's parents' out of season party was a small, plastic reindeer placed next to a spot of green scenery. A small sign on the water tower welcoming the train's passengers to a town they would never truly quit, Obsession. A perfect word for this stranger's and until now, his own imaginary world. Eddy admired the craftsmanship that had gone into constructing this fantasyland. He had purchased his own online at the cost of a few dollars and countless hours of effort.

Eddy envisioned a derailment, a smashed car, a crushed minivan alongside, not underneath, for mayhem obscured was painless. Games require pain of some sort. Would this match of his still be running six months hence? God, he hoped not. What did He think? That was the question? Hamlet had it all wrong. What a self-centered drama prince that one had been. As for himself, the game was becoming familiar, he recognized the signs of an activity going rote. He would not flip indefinitely cards in Solitaire.

The motion of the locomotive led parade was hypnotic, accompanied as it was by the orchestrated soundtrack that enlarged its presence. There was no need for feigned sensitivity. No nemesis existed to be hunted and destroyed.

Why were there no games designed for the hunted. Wasn't that a more common role in life?

Here, in this subterranean world, all was calm and bright, all observers, regardless of age, mesmerized, trusting in the skill of the pre-teen engineer.

Music and intermittent laughter cascaded softly from the main floor of the house but did little to interrupt the joy of the ageless children below.

The party was unusual in having a high turnover rate. Perhaps it was the length of day, or the variety of choices that offered themselves to the residents of Lake Forest on a beautiful summer evening.

It was not the typical "arrive early, stay late suburban affair", but one more frenetic, with a continuous cycling of guests.

Eddy pivoted slowly, made his way nonchalantly to the stairs and silently mounted the carpeted steps. He left the house of summer joy, he himself both ecstatic and disappointed.

Eddy recognized no one as he left, except the youthful conductor and his presumed parents, the hosts.

As he made his exit, he nodded to the new arrivals, maintaining his anonymity through feigned familiarity, their faces as unknown and as forgotten as his would be to them.

If he did not see them as the child's game went...

Eddy departed, unaware of who had come and gone but pleased with his new plan. As he reached his car, Eddy glanced overhead and saw only clouds, their random shape and distribution, managed by unseen forces. Each day was unique, his uncle had claimed, but humans were rewarded for recognizing and living with patterns. Perhaps cloudless days were a condescension to humanity's weakness. Cloudless night too? Eddy asked himself.

In the clouds, folks saw creatures, or the silhouette of a person, sometimes Abe Lincoln in the American skies. It was never anything useful. Could the value be in its uselessness? If that were the case, the modern world was replete with usefulness.

The puffs of vapor encouraged people in their turn to become cloudlike, to waft and move at a relaxed pace, to draw one's attention from the vividness of life with its attendant clashes. A simple upward glance and once was saved from the messiness of existence.

Eddy scanned the sky from east to west, then pivoted ninety degrees and swiveled his head from side to side. He saw neither God nor his uncle.


The park was wonderful in July. It invited visitors to step from its paths. It offered the scent of ferns and evergreens, too full of summer to acquiesce to the perfume of last season's decaying leaves.

Rocks, sharp and irregularly shaped sat patiently underneath, constant as was their fashion, not hesitating to trip the unwary passerby, gifting a sprained ankle as keepsake.

Robert Burnell was not one for nature's tricks. Eddy's uncle sat in a local park, watching a cricket match.

A few tardy clouds drifted by slowly, as if they were intrigued by the awfulness of the human behavior that they saw spread below them.

The game before him lacked the low, repetitious percussion that was his favorite sound in baseball. The regular impact of the ball as it was captured in the mitt, was as pleasant as the less frequent, higher pitched crack when the ball was taken instead by the smooth wood. The sounds were as welcome as the creak of a saddle or the moan of a masted ship, impatient to sail. He enjoyed closing his eyes and turning perception over to his ears. He found it the auditory version of gazing upward on a clear, moonless night, and appreciating what had been present all along.

The sounds were a relief. Alone in his home where music was rarely played, he heard the constant sound of the ocean. He assumed that it was the blood streaming nonstop through his body, likely due to hypertension. It was part of his world, as inescapable as city traffic. He recalled conference stays in the Mandalay Bay resort, where incessant music filled the hotel, the only solitude his room. Even there, his thoughts, his never-ending thoughts and early hints of his elevated blood pressure, were another form of persecution. They were not even voices, simply a hum, the equivalent of a minor, yet chronic ache.

He reopened his eyes and returned to the world of Kentucky cricket under an intense blue sky, the sun itself seeming to have paused to congratulate itself on the day it had created.

The uncle had not learned the rules of the game that was unfolding before him. He was content to watch it uninformed. In his mind understanding undermined appreciation. Things should be accepted as they were.

"Eddy is an ass," he said to himself, before closing his eyes again.

There was the woman that Eddy had mentioned recently and too frequently. He was so smart and so blind, thought the man who watched a game with eyes closed. She was a gold digger, one past her prime. It took one to know one, he admitted without reluctance.

The woman was not right for him. No woman was. It was genetics. Some men were destined to be alone, without family if not friendless. He supposed it was the same for women. The lonely-hearts club was coed and oversubscribed. Kimberly, that was her name, he recalled. She needed to remain in that forlorn organization. It would be better for all concerned. If not, well the gods work in mysterious if not novel ways.

Once back home, he wanted to talk.

Eddy's uncle went through the list of names of friends and family who were worth a call. They were interesting, but they were uniformly dead. Those who remained alive, well they too would be dead sooner or later.

"Why waste the effort?" he asked aloud. A moment later, he frowned, then lifted the phone handset to call Eddy.

The news two days later was the best, exquisite for the media, a triumph of horror over serenity, one that would last for days, and provide local reporters additional exposure with little effort required on their part.

A young boy from Lake Forest had been struck and killed by one of the trains that passed periodically through the upscale neighborhood.

Eddy recognized the boy's photo from the news website. It was indeed the youthful engineer from the party that Eddy had crashed. He was clearly the same boy, even without the engineer's cap, that was now a bitter memory for his parents.

The article stated that the parents had been able to find their son's cap, and quoted the mother, "I don't know if we should bury it with him or burn it and move from this town."

# CHAPTER TWENTY-FOUR

"It can not have been an accident," she said emphatically.

Percheron was there as a show of support, for Percheron lived in the neighborhood, and Zorn was there as support for Percheron.

The mother asked the two detectives, hoping to obtain one honest answer.

Was it one of those hate crimes that you read about?"

"No ma'am," Percheron responded immediately, accompanied a second later by a nod of agreement from the younger man.

Percheron had mastered the art of listening like a woman. He did not prepare responses, he did not anticipate, he did not inadvertently guide the telling. He listened spongelike, not spilling a drop, content in the knowledge that he had time later to reflect and craft a solution.

"This is not the time for conspiracies," the woman told herself firmly.

"What then?" she pursued the pursuers. "Hate, I can understand. It is inside all of us. Believe me, I know. This is...I suppose he must be human as well.

Both men nodded solemnly.

"Detective Percheron and I will help with the investigation. If it is an accident..."

"We were to be laughing today. We would be remembering the party and the fun we had with friends and neighbors."

"Party?"

"And one devil," she added, not hearing the short question.

"You had a party recently? Last night?"

"Yesterday we had Christmas in July."

She noticed their faces; they were expressionless, but they weren't nodding in understanding.

"It's a way to fit in. Everyone in America celebrates Christmas. They say that as well."

After a moment, she added, "This is America." It was said in a tone that matched the detectives' faces, any bitterness invisible.

"We will remember the party very well, for all of the wrong reasons. No more Christmas for us," she said with finality, her voice firm with only a closing sigh that provided a hint of the regret she felt.

Percheron picked up the questioning.

"I'm very sorry, but I must ask you, do you have a list of the guests?"

"We do, but twice the number of people showed up as expected. America is so informal." She said the last sentence as if it was a new discovery.

It could have been three times the number. Americans bring things when they crash a party," the husband added as he joined the small group.

"Like a Trojan Horse," Ash thought.

"We had food and drink left over," he added awkwardly.

"I considered it a great success," the wife said.

"I'm sorry," she blurted, turning and leaving the room.

She had swiveled so abruptly, that a single tear was flung from her cheek, landing silently on the lapel of Percheron's suit coat.

The three men stood quietly for moment, then the father excused himself and followed in the direction of his wife.

"Take a peek into the garage," Percheron commanded Ash, then stood alone.

Ash returned a few minutes later.

"It's big enough for three cars."

"You can learn a lot about a person from their garage."

"Such as what?  We know they are rich."

"And not slobs."

"You looked already?"

"No, but they worked for their money so I anticipated neatness."

"Bingo.  The garage is as neat as a pin.  I work hard for my money, but my living room is not as neat as this garage," he said, pointing to the adjoining door for emphasis.

"Anything else?"

"Was this a test?  Having me look in the garage by myself?"

"What else?"

"They don't do yard work."

"No lawn tractor?"

"Nope."

"You pass. That means another suspect."

"Suspect?"

"I cannot accept that this was an accident," Percheron said, echoing the distraught mother's words.

# CHAPTER TWENTY-FIVE

"'Boy killed by train.' That is what the paper says."

The full size locomotive had sliced the boy's previously unscarred body into a flesh and bloodied nightmare that would chill all whose job it was to view such horrors for the rest of their careers, and beyond.

Percheron sighed.

"Trains and boys. Boys like trains. I did. What about you Ash?"

"I suppose so."

"Real trains, a boy's imagination is enough ticket to ride for free. His mother said that he and his dad had quite the model setup in the basement. Those are real too, in their own way. Now it's all video games."

"I had a one now that I think of it. A railroad robbery game."

"Video games without touch or smell, or taste."

"I didn't like it much. You can only rob a train so many ways."

"With sixty percent of your senses cut off, I'm surprised you could rob it at all."

"I suppose that may be another reason I didn't play it very often."

"And now this boy is killed."

"In a senseless accident. Was the boy deaf?"

Percheron frowned at the question.

"No. Hell Ash, you were there at the interview."

"Sorry."

"Me too. He wasn't deaf and it wasn't an accident."

"Good God, surely not suicide. Not at that age. A few years older, maybe."

Percheron frowned again, this time at the sentiment his colleague expressed, for it was valid.

"Murder?" The word uttered softly.

"Yes. Here is the report on what passed for an autopsy. The head was...intact. More or less. The rest was as gruesome as you can imagine. The photos are obscene in their clarity. Someone had the bright idea to X-ray the head. See for yourself."

The younger detective steeled himself, glanced at the wastepaper can to verify its location, and then looked at the medical film.

"A bullet. A bullet? The boy was shot? Of course he was. Sorry. Thank God that someone had the initiative to do the X-ray. Otherwise, this would have been written off as a tragic accident."

"Or thank the devil. An accidental death would have been kinder to the family."

"But kinder to the killer as well, Perch."

"Maybe it would been worth it."

"Do you think so?"

"No, I don't."

"You sound angry."

"Sometimes anger helps, there must a reason why we have it. Sometimes it helps us, sometimes it doesn't."

Ash was pleased to hear himself referred to as a member of us and missed Perch's next comment.

"What?" he forced himself to ask.

Percheron repeated himself, his mouth a straight line, his muscles weary of frowning.

"It's hard to determine when anger helps and when it hurts. The anger of others keeps us employed. Do you suppose so?"

"Yes, I suppose so."

Percheron smiled.

"I was angry. Maybe it focused me, particularly when I read the ballistics report. Two pieces of information from this terrible death: murder by gunshot, a .22 short, and a possible match to a shell casing found near the body at Portland cemetery.

"The report doesn't say that. They found no bullet in the Portland body."

The pair stood there, considering the possibilities.

"Did they find a shell case in Lake Forest?"

"No one looked."

"I guess we can organize a search."

"No."

"No?"

Ash did not wait for an explanation.

"You think the killer missed at Portland and used a club of some sort?"

Percheron nodded.

"Only you and I know this. Two murders, one gun."

"We don't have definitive evidence. We have one bullet and one shell casing from separate scenes."

"In an odd enough caliber that they might very well be linked."

"One murderer?"

"I hope so. And I hope not."

"Which way do we go, Perch?"

"There are so many guns, but most of them are larger caliber."

"We hypothesize one killer?"

"I'm glad you know the big words. It sounds better than we flipped a coin."

"We," the young detective thought. Partners now in this hunt, for better or worse. He didn't know if he dreaded or prayed for the return of Detective Ertras, Perch's regular partner. Was she lucky or cursed to miss this show. On that matter he offered himself no hypothesis.

# CHAPTER TWENTY-SIX

She mistreated the taps and had a heretical disregard for the proper pouring of a beer. Ritual was lost, spillage unimportant. That lack of concern would not rescue the planet from whatever crisis was in fashion. She would not receive much as a tip. Percheron expected that his beer, which he limited to two, be delivered correctly.

On the other hand, the bartender had a way of walking, an insouciant locomotion in her step, that soothed all but the most meticulous of customers. Of course, she was tattooed, a condition to which he had recently resigned himself. It was a fetish, and her markings made her safe, or so he speculated.

But there were other, less selective killers. There was a murderer for every flavor of victim.

A spin around town, like the hands of an old-fashioned clock, or the horses at Churchill, destined to end where one began. But he could escape. He had only to continue along the interstate. All he needed was within reach, his wallet and cellphone sat in his pockets. That was sufficient for a modern man. The interstate touched the entire country. There really was only one road. The country was large, he would not need to stop by home for his passport.

It was exhilarating. Boredom would be left behind as he sped, or crawled, it would be indifferent to him. Equally meaningless was direction. East, West, South, North, they were interchangeable.

"No!' Eddy shouted as he rejected the temptation that offered itself beyond the windshield. It was merely a larger oval.

He nearly slammed on the brakes, to bring the farce to an end, but a quick glance in the rearview mirror convinced him otherwise. Instead, he pivoted his ankle, depressing the accelerator in anger at his own indecision. Just as quickly he eased up on the right pedal, his racing mind slowing in tandem with the car, both machines following the path of least resistance.

That night, as Eddy sought sleep, he questioned his two aborted decisions. To press forward or lock his brakes, either would have meant his not drifting off here in the comfort of home.

He might be dead, with no concern for the fate of the driver who had been behind him, or he might be alive elsewhere, whatever that entailed. Eddy would sleep. Sleep was riskless, its own sort of circular pause. Sleep was elsewhere.

Just before he lost consciousness, Eddy thought again of the innocent driver. Caring about others, that was what defined humanity. Wasn't it? No, that was silly. It was not the life of a stranger that had shifted Eddy's foot from one pedal to another.

Eddy did not want to die.

The next morning dawned, a day much like the one before it. Similar enough to the preceding twenty-four hours, that the average person would not have noticed. Some people had died, others had arrived to begin their time on the prison's stage. The world was more or less as it had been, the day destined to be as unremarkable as any other.

# CHAPTER TWENTY-SEVEN

The detectives were accustomed to eating lunch on angry stomachs.

"Crime is continually out of hand. We struggle to keep it out of sight. These are deliberate, disgusting attempts to provoke a reaction."

"The press hasn't raised the alarm."

"The press it not what they once thought that they were."

"Were they ever?"

"My point is that reporters live on a hair trigger, hoping to derive fame and fortune from the misery of some and the morbidness (morbidity) of many.

Ash took a sip of water to hide his discomfort at the description that could apply to himself.

"They expect to have the wealth to be interred in Cave Hill, as they see the subject of their stories confined to some lesser zip code."

Percheron drank from his own glass of water.

"What confuses me is the killer."

"You mean that he should be seeking fame and fortune, well, fame, as well?"

"Yes. But not a peep."

"Maybe he knows that we will catch him. He's seen the shows."

"Which shows?"

"Forensic files, for example. If he's local he must have heard of you."

"Don't flatter me. I'm less well known than a third assistant coach in girls' lacrosse at U of L."

It was the younger man's turn to shrug.

"If he is from out of town, again, he must have seen these types of television programs. So, he is resigned to being caught."

"Or not."

"Or not?"

"I am beginning to think that he simply does not care."

"About being apprehended?"

"Yes. We like to think that serial killers are A players, and that they think of us the same way. I wonder if this is a game of solitaire."

"In what way?"

"I don't know. Our participation is not encouraged but not discouraged either. We have had no communication, either directly or through an intermediary. He is doing his thing, and if we are there to watch or not is immaterial. This person will not help us to catch him. He does not want fame."

"But the bodies are all left in public view."

They appear to be unconnected. Each is tragic in its own way. As I said, the press is none the wiser, and I fear that while we may be one step ahead of them, we may have advanced in the wrong direction."

"It makes us both angry," Ash stated the obvious.

"We find ourselves surrounded by sinners Ash. We don't preach to them, We don't offer to forgive them. We don't seek to change them. We arrest them."

"You have been to the funerals. You have heard the eulogies. You have heard that these were all good people. You have seen the interviews and the background checks. All good people. You have come to same conclusion?"

"I have."

He paused.

"On the other hand, no one is an angel."

"Angels don't have funerals. They've had eons to eradicate their faults."

"I would need even longer," Ash said with a grin.

"It makes me think of one thing."

"Who?"

"Yes. Who. And why?"

"That's two, Perch."

"Math is hard. That's one of my faults," Perch replied with his own brand of grin.

"But murder may not be so hard."

"Oh?" Ash asked, anxious to hear Perch's reasoning."

"It's not hard when there are so many clues."

Ash protested,

"So many clues? If we had three of them, we would be drowning in evidence."

"I'm referring to the crimes themselves, specifically the victims' goodness."

"There is nothing in common. A few overlaps in acquaintances and friends. But these have all been checked and doublechecked. Zilch."

"They'd have liked each other."

"Yeah. I suppose."

"Do you like me?"

The younger man blushed.

Percheron repeated the question.

"Yeah, sure Perch."

"Why?" Percheron asked, pressing the line of questioning.

He did not let the embarrassment last and answered his own question.

"The victims would have liked each other because, despite their religious differences, they shared a faith. Weird? Many victims can be as annoying in life as their killers are. That is not true here."

Ash shrugged.

"We have a similar passion to solve crimes, to keep strangers safe."

"All people are good people some point in life. The victims were all good."

The detectives understood that Life is a ruleless game if one paid the slightest attention.

"And we are too."

"There are degrees of goodness."

"That is very modern thinking, Perch," the younger detective said, still uncomfortable using the man's nickname to his face.

Percheron indicated nothing to show disapproval.

"Let's see where all this goodness can take us."

"These brutal killings have nothing in common. Do you think they are related?"

"Yes."

"A kook?"

Percheron shrugged.

"Maybe."

"Kooks brag. Eventually."

"We aren't the audience."

"Who is? The media. As far as I know, no media has been contacted. Not staged, no shared m.o."

"The victims were all good people. These crimes confuse and frighten the public. This is not one drug deal gone well for one criminal, bad for the other, where the roles could have been reversed."

"Four good church going people. I say church, but the doctor was Jewish, the boy, Muslim."

"No atheists?"

"I don't think so. They are pretty rare."

"They might be hesitant to advertise. It may be worth pursuing."

"Agreed. I'll leave that to you. Good luck."

"Is this a test?"

"To see how I react? Like me and tango. I have a method to determine if tango can lead to more. Is a woman willing to be led while staying silent. You must have something similar for your rookies."

"You are not a rookie."

"You know what I mean."

"Sure. You're the first to mention it. As to the tango, how does your method work out for you?"

"It usually crashes as soon as the music stops and the rules are suddenly rewritten. As if someone flipped a railroad switch."

"There was no switch involved here," Perch said as he abruptly rerouted the conversation back to the murder of the boy.

"My grandfather used to work for L&N railroad. He helped me to set up my train set."

Tango and train sets, Percheron observed.

"You would be surprised how much the two have in common. As I was saying...".

Percheron sat down and sipped from his tea. He looked relaxed, yet he frowned at the younger man's words.

"Usually the woman is ready to reset the rules after three minutes of silence. She may be a great dancer, but that marks the end of any relationship. Its quick and painless. We may even dance again, but... That may not be life but it is my life."

Percheron nodded, once again reminded that most people inhabited a world larger than his. Was he a zookeeper or just another exhibit, he wondered.

"Something is off."

"Something is always off. Off is what we fix."

"Its off more with this case than the others."

"All of them?"

"Many of them."

"He doesn't care? They both knew that the he of interest was Eddy."

"He doesn't care more than most."

"Eddy is playing with you. You must have seen that behavior hundreds of time. We all have. You more than anyone. This is Eddy's first game and your what, five hundredth."

Perch smiled at the exaggeration. He thought for a moment, then responded,

"This is not his first game."

"He has a criminal record? How did I miss that?"

"I mean that he plays games. He even created one, it made him his fortune. He's clean."

"Games are games?" the other man asked, not sure himself what his words were intended to say.

"Games are games," Perch repeated, and his colleague worried that he would be asked to explain. Instead, the older man complimented him.

"That is the best question today. If the answer is yes? I wonder."

"Our game is justice," Ash said, feeling as if he were responding to a child's question and show and tell. "Half the jurors believe in ghosts or UFOs. Some in both," he added.

"No, those are usually the defendants. The most accurate memories are the ones that are never recalled. The law is like the Colonnade," Percheron observed to his colleague, referring to the well known basement cafeteria in downtown Louisville that had recently closed. "It attracted a large crowd, but no one liked every dish. People pick and choose what they like from among the offerings. And then one day, either their tastes change..."

"Or their mores."

"Mores, great word."

"I went to Shakespeare in the park."

"Alone?"

"No. I had an alibi."

"I see," Percheron replied, aware that his colleague's private life was just that.

"Anyway, people get tired of a long-term city tradition, and poof, the Colonnade closes."

"Too many laws that a person doesn't like..."

156

"And they chuck them all. Like I said, no one enjoys the entire menu. All that is required is a nudge when they are perched on a tipping point."

Percheron thought again of his own tipping point. He had no issue accepting that today was not yesterday and that tomorrow would not be today. But there comes a day when no tomorrows would resemble any of his yesterdays.

# CHAPTER TWENTY-EIGHT

Percheron sat at the small bar in Mark's Feed Store, sipping his iced tea that had already been placed in a go cup. He had stopped by for a brisket sandwich, a meal in itself that packed calories to keep him going all night if necessary. He would compliment it with greens on his next day off. While he waited for his takeaway order, he studied the huge flag that covered the west wall of the rustic restaurant. He wondered if a given star represented a particular state, then grunted at the ridiculousness of his question.

The symbol carried fifty five-pointed stars, arranged in alternating even/odd quantities, the same number as long as he could remember. Thank God for big favors.

A few things were constant, but they were in the minority. Years ago, if you hadn't had complaints lodged against, you needed to get off your ass and care more. Times change, as did rules and law. He was grateful that he was stuck, if that was the right word, in homicide. Murder was still wrong, that was something all the stars aligned on.

A few stools away, two elderly gentlemen were discussing their afternoon on the golf course. Valhalla, Percheron concluded based on their dress and language. Golf, another possibility for his upcoming retirement. It was a gentil sport, despite its need for personal coaches, chiropractors, and spinal surgeons. Would sixth hole psychics be next, he mused.

No, golf was not for him. Other than brutal death wrapped in misleading clues was for him?

On the other hand, gentil was not bad for a retired cop. Golf was an otherworldly concept, as far removed from normal life as his own workplace, if in the opposite direction. The game itself clean, honest, played in a quiet, designed with an idyllic environment, with only a tinge of frustration that could be brushed away that it was merely a pastime. It was more akin to Heaven's waiting room than was any air-conditioned, carpeted hospice.

He lifted the order, measuring its accuracy by weight, not contents. As he walked up the steep, back parking lot, he smiled. Golf was nice, but he had work to do.

His was a hobby disguised as career, a pastime while confined. He would have one when he was sentenced to retirement. It would be one of his own choosing, more than one if he liked. Would it be like prison woodshop without blades, or acting lessons for convicted confidence men?

Either way, it would be a life sentence, as escape proof as any human creation. Dance, travel, language lessons, some other weekly drug? It was cheaper to sleep and just dream.

In the car the radio was playing a song he liked, one with enough gaps between lyrics to permit him to think.

Percheron spent the rest of the daylight hours alone with his thoughts.

As the afternoon turned late, the weather turned. Percheron drove slowly through the summer rainstorm, the metronome of the car's wipers a reminder that some things were still reliable. Off to the right, he noticed a man standing alone under an opened umbrella in a cemetery. The man faced away from the road, unmoving before a gravestone.

"A parent, a child, a lover, a friend," Perch wondered, the words forming in his mind in rhythm with the sweeping wipers. All grief looks the same at distance, he said to himself, then refocused on his destination.

The man stood alone under the umbrella, the chatter of the rain on the black nylon incomprehensible. It was as if voices of the surrounding dead were speaking all at once, not at him, but amongst themselves. He felt himself a wedding crasher. He walked away quickly.

I don't believe in anything. But when I place flowers on her grave, or I speak to the grass that covers her, I pretend that is her attending me, and I can believe, almost, that it's important.

Perch gave a final glance at the unknown mourner.

"I want to be left alone is uttered in despair as often as I want someone," he thought.

Later, as alone as the unknown mourner, Percheron sat before his television. Too much true crime; relived and televised. What was the value of a hobby to pass the time. Alcohol required less effort and a quorum was at hand. Death, violence in hindsight: equal parts unnecessary and regret.

The murder itself dissected and presented in detail between sponsor mandated recesses, slices aimed at viewers, targeted to fill the imagined voids in their own lives. Such a lag between crime and punishment.

He was outnumbered, overwhelmed, with no cavalry over the horizon.

Paradoxically, advertisements for alarms, firearms, guard dogs, and other similar accoutrements of a secured residence were absent from the publicities. Was the typical consumer of death television completely stocked up or simply filled with despair.

Perch flipped from channel to channel, before settling on off, its content as equally illuminating as the others.

He picked up the French hardcover comic book that he had purchased at a seller's table in Paristown. He chuckled to himself. Something old and something new. Was a return to the black and white of colored comics a valid pastime if he married it to learning a second language? Only his opinion counted

He had bought the book on a whim. It had reminded him of his short trip to Rose Hill and of a case he had not been asked to investigate, let alone solve. It was the same day that he had seen the bizarre bulletin board notice for some sort of in person game.

He turned the pages in the thin book, following the pictures, not comprehending the language.

His country was in the midst of a virtual revolution, shifting odder and odder, and according to the law enforcement literature he read, it was bleeding over into real life, real crime, like an unstoppable pestilence from the Middle Ages.

Expect failure. Its arrival won't disappoint you was law enforcement's consensus.

# CHAPTER TWENTY-NINE

Percheron regarded thoughtfully the kid at a nearby table. He was on his cellphone, while his parents scanned the sparse menu. The boy was thumbing the screen, composing a text of unknown content, destined momentarily for a contact anonymous to the guardians sitting inches away.

It was the boy's dextrous use of his opposing digits that amazed the detective. It was evolution in plain sight. The few times Percheron had attempted the same maneuver, he came quickly to appreciate the phrase "all thumbs".

How was that possible he had wondered in bewilderment. His niece, residing between her uncle and this boy in age, had made the transition from fingers as enthusiastically as he had not. She was a burning convert to the slim device. It was appropriately called an apple.

He had resigned himself to staying in his own snake infested garden. It was comfortable, if not safe. But his role in the town he called home would change.

Retire, retirement, retired. Retire, it involved retreat. Was that peace or defeat? Two sides of a coin that until now did not sit heavily in his pocket, its lesser mass not heavier than his Glock and other tools of his protective trade.

Percheron recognized his own melancholy for what it was, as did the former colleagues he seemed to stumble across more and more often like too many ghosts of Christmas future in an inaccurately cast production of Carol. Their conversations, filled with all important silences, belied the gaps that remained in their exciting, new lives.

As quickly as it had arrived, the oppressive melancholy passed.

These murders, this case, it was senseless, deliberately provocative, like a brutal gang initiation. It was indecent, in a world where the term itself had increasingly higher bars to surpass in order to be appropriate. It was reserved for the most heinous, the most biblical of crimes. Was this a religious crime, a war of attack and counterattack?

God forbid, he thought. That doesn't happen in America! Or it hasn't until now, he reasoned. Booze, broads, and bucks; was the bible making a fourth at the suspect table? Religious wars? This is America, the new world. Act like it! He wanted to scream at the unknown perpetrators. Instead, Percheron himself focused on the idea of a new world.

Would it be worthwhile to consult a few religious leaders? No, not leaders, but those a step beneath. Believers were what he needed. The man in the pew, so to speak. Despite the horror of his theory, Percheron felt an immense sense of relief.

He thought back to an earlier crime, decades in the past. He had traveled to Pennsylvania where he had consulted with psychics. It had been a good idea at the wrong time, and the trip had provided no tangible benefit, other than a lesson to be open minded. The scene had been rural, farms and forests. And deer.

Percheron had smelled the all too familiar odor a few seconds before he realized the purpose of the totally unfamiliar sight unfolding before him. A pickup truck was slowing onto the road's shoulder. A deer lay dead there, and the driver stopped expertly before the carcass. The bed of the truck contained two or three other dead deer, the count soon to be augmented by one. Sufficient road deaths to warrant creating a part time job. Bring out your dead, he thought of the ways chanted during the plague of centuries ago. Percheron had noticed that the truck's occupants wore pistols to finish any unfortunate victims. His life was death. His work was death.

How many murders had been committed since that long ago sejour in Rose Hill? Percheron preferred to not tally the count. What good was it? How many had he solved, as if that mattered. He excelled at a job that should not exist. What value it had was losing its worth, save for those few who visited the graves on birthdays. Did undetected killers commemorate the loss another way, on another day? Did they like to see the grass and stone result of their sin? Sin, where did that word spring from? He really was getting old. His vocabulary had aged to match his wardrobe. Sin? They were criminals, by and in his book. He would leave decisions on sin to believers. Yes, he would need to listen to a few of the faithful. He would speak to his niece. She was of dating age and must know one or two young believers.

# CHAPTER THIRTY

"I don't have the time."

"What are you doing instead? Chasing another murderer?"

"It's important."

"So is life Uncle Perch. We only have each other."

"You will find someone. It isn't difficult."

"Not if you are searching a killer. You haven't found anyone for yourself. Someone normal."

"You are still young."

"So are you. In your own way. What about Ertras?"

"Castorina?"

"Yeah."

"What about her? She is on vacation, she can't go this play you mentioned, either."

"Not the play. Thats not for a few weeks. I meant you and she..."

"We could what?"

"You know for a detective you can be blind."

"I'm not blind. Castorina is your age. I'd be more open to dating your boyfriend's widowed mother."

"Which boyfriend?"

"That is your first clue, detective."

"I can see me asking every first date if their mother is a widow. Once they learn I'm a homicide detective, they won't stick around to finish their

Starbucks. It is only a play, three hours tops for the entire evening. Just you and I, no surprises on my part."

"I heard that there was more to the people involved in the play than just..."

"My partner, he has his own agenda."

"Suspicious?"

"Simply because the director's wife is well known he thinks that he can use our involvement to leverage his career."

"I'll think about it."

"What are you doing instead?"

"That isn't the point. I don't enjoy murder mysteries. I have plenty on the job, and whatever quota is lacking, comes to me when I'm sleeping. I don't care to see any in between."

Percheron enjoyed seeing his niece. He had considered Noche, a Mexican restaurant that had replaced a church for those seeking more spice before eternity arrived. It was not the place for a serious conversation.

Instead, he had been fortunate to reserve the table next to the immense oak at Captain's Quarter. Sitting beside it watching the boats of various sizes and purposes, all for pleasure, as they quietly, wakelessly, entered and exited the river and their moorings at the yacht club, the pair resembled a father and daughter on an outing. Across the water lay magnificent homes on the Indiana shore. Upstream, the new bridge, under construction and as of yet unnamed, rose just as silently, its builders gone for the evening.

Emily Muse wondered if this was the fate that awaited her, immersed in a world of never-ending nightmares. She wondered what her uncle would do once he retired in a few weeks, when the nightmares continued yet he had lost the means to vanquish them.

"The fact that the Muslim boy was murdered is not public information."

Emily nodded.

His faith was not mentioned by the press, whose skill at self-censorship grew while they mantrad freedom of the press. It was noted by the police who understood the practicalities of a job. They were professionals, not experts.

"One doesn't think of American children as religious. They age into unreason. Faith is a voluntary vice, one that comes at the year when one may vote and choose other self-harms."

Emily knew all about harm. Like her colleagues, she had discovered victims in all their foibles and frailties. Under the glare of morgue lights or the victim's investigator, all secrets were disclosed to Perch and his ilk. From financial records to hidden tattoos to sexual preferences an investigation was a sequence of dates that began poorly and proceeded downhill.

He autopsied their life. As for the actual murderer and understudy suspects auditioned along the way, their lives too were dissected and examined before any public trial. It was a process that offered a taste of final judgment to faithful and infidel alike.

Percheron described the boy's funeral.

He had seen larger turnouts he supposed but could not remember when. There was a distinct absence of the boy's contemporaries as he had been of an age where parents lied to their children. Santa was surely real, and death, why that did not exist if it could be hidden from their eyes.

Perch thought of normal funerals, the deceased aged, the majority of their friends already awaiting them in whatever fashion one envisioned the long-departed waiting for new arrivals.

"What can I do to help?" Emily asked her uncle.

"I heard that same question asked recently by one of the mourners of a widow. I still remember her answer. She used to be on radio, she has that sort of voice. It was full of emotion, but perfectly enunciated.

'Unless you can raise the dead, there is nothing you can do.'

Me I don't know what I believe about raising the dead. It would put me out of a job. That might be the best trade in history. Until then, I will try to give them justice. You might call it revenge for the family but that is the only gift I can offer. That is what I can do to help. I'd like you to talk with a few of the folks on our list. Unofficially and unidentified."

"Understood."

"Strange," Percheron commented again on the funeral.

"It's refreshing."

Emily regarded her uncle in disbelief.

"It's not like a funeral for an old person, where the mourners resemble a collection of actors who failed the audition for the role of the deceased."

Emily frowned in agreement.

"Let's order and talk of happier things."

## CHAPTER THIRTY-ONE

The walker woke, smiling at the sunlight that streamed in through the window's opened drapes, detoured but not deterred by the inexpensive foldable screen that stood erect between the pane of glass and the firm mattress on which she lay.

She followed the orb's lead, rising to her feet, frowning only for one pace when she thought of the murder investigation. It was regrettable, a tragedy for the family, but it was in the past, as vanished as yesterday's sunset. It was burned away, extinguished, forgettable if not yet forgotten. Like the sun, she would blaze her own trail, both literally and figuratively. Emerald would return to Joe Creason park.

# CHAPTER THIRTY-TWO

"Life is nothing but a bigger version of high school. I'm not gonna get married." Ash had been told that by two men whom he had served as best man.

The date had a meaningless job. He was beginning to appreciate the case ringing in his mind like an insistent snooze alarm.

Blessed with no after-hours concerns regarding her own work, she was quick to notice his distraction, but not it's source.

He did like that about her, and he already enjoyed being her center. He would relish the experience throughout their brief time together. He had determined that she was not his center.

That experience was not novel; quickly meeting and rejecting a woman as a long-term commitment, often before the main course arrived. It was why he had switched to ordering the smallest and least expensive entrée.

Not the right woman for him, he had told himself often enough. He had hoped several times that he was wrong, that the person across the table from him was the right culprit, woman, he corrected himself.

This girl, woman he repeated silently, she was nice. As always, there was something lacking, the same crucial bit of evidence that was missing in this most personal of cases. Friends disappoint eventually, as did his dates. He must have someone wise divulge that secret to him.

She spoke in a whisper. Was she ill? Chronically secretive? Addicted to romance novels? Allure withered into annoyance. He smiled at her unheard comment, his mind clear to focus on tomorrow.

An image of Perch's niece sprang into his mind. It was undoubtedly wrong in every aspect, as he had never met Emily Muse, he knew nothing about her, except her being a young woman, a detective. He would conduct his own off-hours, more or less, investigation. Louisville was and would be home and it was time to be serious about more than career.

Crime and punishment, detectives and criminals came and went. There had to be more to life.

I am suspicious by paycheck, Ash Zorn thought. At times he even suspected himself, he joked. More worrisome, his mentor. Or his boss, or partner. It depended on the moment. Perch could wear three hats simultaneously. This case was going nowhere, and the bodies were piling up like one of those PBS British mysteries that intrigued his grandmother. If I solve this case, I'll get my own TV show, Ash fantasized. That would impress Gran. He came back to Earth. There was no well written script to follow, only police procedure and the occasional forensic evidence. More often it was sifting the statements from witness. Sober or intoxicated, they were equally unobservant. Ash Zorn returned from his daydream, put the depressing thoughts away and went to shave and dress for his disappointing date.

The date had not gone as Ash had anticipated. His sister had arranged it, and she had likely counselled the date, Haleigh, to steer the conversation toward work.

"Are you complaining or bragging, Ash", Haleigh asked.
"He takes it too seriously."
"Personally?"
I wouldn't say that exactly. It isn't like he's affronted that people are being killed when he is on duty, hell he is always on duty. It is not a challenge, you know catch me if you can."
"You've told me what it is not. You haven't told me what it is. Remember we aren't all cops and criminals. I'm neither, you know."
"Do you take your job seriously?"
"Sure."
"But at the end of the day, it is just a job."
"Sure. It is fun at times."
"Perch doesn't stop. Murder is a puzzle that he must solve as quickly as possible."
"I suppose that time is critical in police work. Its life and death."
"I know that."
"He has nothing else."
"Have you met Perch?"

"In a way. I have met his counterpart in companies. And elsewhere. He is a type."

"I would like to see someone say to Perch, Detective Percheron, you are a type."

"He knows it. He has said that to himself for years."

"Are you a psychologist now?"

"Aren't we all a bit? You especially, Ash."

He liked the way she said his name.

"Why me especially?"

"You become what you do. It works so easily on men. You have only to look at the military, any career in fact. You become what you do."

"I don't like the sound of that."

Her shrug was accompanied with a slight smile, ready to speak of something else.

"On the other hand, you may be on to something. That might explain why..."

"Why what?"

"Why Perch is always providing me with opportunities to do something other than work."

"Like what?" Haleigh asked cautiously.

"Free time. Family events, beers with the guys."

"Like tonight?"

"No, not like tonight."

"Your detective knows that there is more to life than death."

"But not for him?" Ash asked, realizing the answer.

"He doesn't want you to follow in his footsteps. He is being kind to you."

Ash thought that this was definitely not the usual date. Simultaneously, he was not sure that he wanted kindness if that meant not following in the footsteps of the city's most accomplished detective. More to life than being a legend? A well-rounded life as a mediocre investigator? There was room for both. Still, what would he want chiseled on his own tombstone? Would it matter? No one visited cemeteries anymore. Whether the dead had family or not, they were equally alone in their grave.

"He is doing you a favor with the time off. Enjoy it."

"I can't. I have chores tonight."

"But you just got through telling me that he is cutting you tons of slack."

"Not tonight. Not on these cases."

"Cases?"

"This case. Hey, I gotta go."

"Are you sure, Ash?"

He really did like sound of his name on her lips.

# CHAPTER THIRTY-THREE

Kim thought of her crown, touching it delicately with her tongue. Her hopeful probing, in the desire that the foreign object might only be a dream, an imaginary, vaporous fantasy that might disappear at her touch. It was there, fixed in place, permanent. The crown was her first, and it would be her last she lied to herself.

Lies and women; she thought of her dad. Her father had told her, ad nauseum, the only Latin she cared to remember, that women overestimated their ability to judge character. Whether it was a serpent's, their own, or that of a man, women failed. Consistently, they failed. Women failed. Women failed. It was a chorus that he would have led, happily, in weekly services.

She thought now that poor judgment was an attribute that natural selection should have eliminated by now. With a shudder, she thought that women proved God's existence. She laughed immediately, delighted that her father had not reached the same conclusion during his lifetime. She guffawed in imagining that he had, but he had been caught in a paradox that not even death would permit him to ignore. His own belief made it obsolete. Oh well, men fail too, she thought, a smile on her lips.

Her smile froze when she thought of Eddy.
He puzzled her. Their first "date" with a stopover at
a church had been a shock. It was so unexpected
and yet being driven to a church was such a familiar
if distant experience. A long-ago memory that she
had striven to erase. She had nearly bolted from
Eddy's car and called for Uber. Oh, if it had been so
easy all those years ago.

She had no desire to have a religious man in
her life again. She had stayed in the car and only
accompanied Eddy into the church when he had
made no effort to convince her. The unanticipated
stop had startled her. Being ignored had irritated
her and banished her fear.

She should take him to the Corner Café. If
he hated it, perfect.

And if he liked it? Well, that would not be
terrible either. Her smile thawed and widened.

Don't forget where you came from.

I remember why I left.


Kimberly thought of the two men currently in
her life, not of the dozens who had occupied it, and
preoccupied her, over the years.

A few names she still recalled, despite her
best efforts to scrub them from her memory. There
was no exercise to excise memories, except
alcoholism, and that was worse than the periodic
reappearance of unpleasant recollections, like old
relatives who refused to die but complained of their
maladies at each reunion.

Eddy and Craig. They were opposites to one another. Surely that meant that one of them was perfect for her.

Choosing one could not help but create a missed opportunity. They were both affluent, and that was not to be missed. One was hands on, the other cerebral.

Kimberly twisted her mouth to one side. She had to be harsh, she was of an age where it was a regular outfit in her life, especially on evenings like tonight, when she was alone, behind closed doors. Or she could flip a coin. She had tried that once, no twice. She was not a gambler; any decision would be hers alone. Eddy was odd, but so was she. Too weird for each other? Probably. But it was a good weird. He played games, Craig played with cars.

Boys never grew up! They still believed in the magic one was surrounded by as children. She needed magic, she needed to decide. Getting both to commit would be child's play and smiled at her own momentary return to the past. Harsh was sweet.

She could have a future with either of them. As to her past, her famous friend Annacine had told her that she one couldn't escape one's past.

"I can confine it to a corner of my future, ignored. I will refuse to ever clean that section, and it will eventually disappear under the dust," Kimberly had replied confidently.

## CHAPTER THIRTY-FOUR

The victim's loved one sat in the curtained darkness of her bedroom. Although it was night, the curtain had been closed for days, the woman angry at the sun for its cheerfulness, the certainty of its arrival. She was resentful of the children who played outside in its warmth, their intermittent squeals and happy screams unintentionally mocking her, the sound muffled but not blocked by the luxuriant window coverings.

She tried to think of nothing, concentrating to her utmost to simply exist, plantlike. It proved impossible, and she wondered if vegetation was as mindless as she envisioned. Everything was upside down, unimportant, meaningless.

She wanted to sleep, her mind that is. Her body was resistant; it had slept too long, while her mind knew that it would never sleep enough again.

Annie was again at Starbucks. She hated to reconsider. Therapists repeated the word as a mantra. Reconsideration had ruined her life. She sat placidly, anger warming the pleasant, chilled, silent atmosphere of the café. It wouldn't last.

How she had wished that she could have been preggo forever. She loved how chic the word sounded. As for preggo itself, its discomfort was offset by the feeling. How had her psychiatrist put it so long ago, "You crave the prestige without the responsibility, Annie." He used her name to make sure she got his point. Well, she got his point, the goody two shoes. He sat there and listened to patients' stories and dreams because he had none of her own. But she didn't say anything to him. She knew that he was right, but one learned early on to not tell the truth.

Where would the world be without lies all around? She had been polite, she had not ridiculed him with the truth of his mundane life, hearing of excitement secondhand. Now, she had never seen him again, well, only once. She had made her point then when she left in the middle of their last session.

Annie sipped her warm drink. She had drank better.

Starbucks would go airline on its customers. Reduced portions, higher prices, fewer amenities, smaller and harder seats. Signs were already in evidence.

She remembered the coffee in Hawaii, when she had gone to the island state with her late husband. He did not enjoy the coffee, nor the flight, for he had gone to Maui as carry-on luggage. He half-filled the urn, one that had been on sale due to its odd, larger than normal size. People did not want to remember the departed as dearly as they claimed. She had discovered that immediately.

There was plenty of room in the urn, he had no legs or shoulders or head to enjoy it, and instead his ashes were jostled and shaken by the constant motion, so that upon landing, his remains were even less recognizable. He would have no earthly grave, for those were long term rentals, a constant reminder that he retained a permanent address.

Instead, he would go to sea, he had always hated water, but Annie had always wanted to go to Hawaii. They had compromised, she had pretended that he would have he wanted, while Annie had decided, that he, well, he simply wasn't.

It had been a mistake, for each glance at the magnificent waters of the Pacific was a constant reminder of him. She should have dumped the urn in Jersey.

That was all in the past, this was Louisville.

Canada. They had no guns in the north. She would be ok with her knife. Crime flourished everywhere and she needed protection. A girl had constant need of protection.

Canada. They had no guns, but they had the northern lights. That sounded cool. It was probably free, or low cost for low people like her.

Her mind flickered to the young detective. He has a lot to learn. He is the one that should reconsider. As for me, I'm done here.

It was the height of summer. Warm days beckoned her north as if she were a bird. A penniless snowbird. She reminded herself to play the Powerball. Despite her condition, she might still have some luck left.

No more nightmares over what one person could do to another in less time than it took to apologize. She had seen too much cruelty. Leaving a corpse in a cemetery was downright polite in her experience.

One piece of luck was all she needed, Annie said to herself and God. She pictured the customers at the local Thornton's, supplicants queued in front of the Powerball machine.

She had managed until now, migrating like a bird, sleeping in parks, and cemeteries like countless species of birds. Was she less deserving than a sparrow?


Emerald sat on the rented chair, watching the rented television. Only the news was free, and it was not worth the price. There was no mention of the murder in the park, her murder, she had come to think of it. Other killings, equally random it seemed, had come to take precedence, like more recent lighting strikes in a never-ending storm.

Maybe Louisville had not been such a wise move, she thought. Her gaze flitted around the room, furnished by some soulless private equity firm she surmised. It struck her as being a cell in a minimum-security prison. Likely the same corporate management, she supposed, extinguishing the broadcast before it offered its vignette of joyful news. Emerald wished that she had someone whom she could telephone. There was no one.

Emerald had been invited to play pickleball by one of the men in her apartment complex. But she was now wary of forming any new ties, however casual. Louisville was dangerous. That much was obvious. And those detectives. Police were the same everywhere, including television; overworked but conscientious. With the murder in the park, she no longer felt safe. The older detective—what an odd name, Percheron—his distinguished looks forced her to suppose that he was good at his job. He had assured her she was in no danger. That was silly on the face of it. And if she were called as a witness. That might be years from now. He had not offered her protection, only words. And this new man, the pickler, was that all he was? A protector, or a threat? Or simply a friendly neighbor? Maybe she should buy a gun. A gun she could be sure of. Just in case.

# CHAPTER THIRTY-FIVE

More often than not on his day off, Percheron would write down what he should devote that day to, place the transcribed task in an old cigar box that was nearly filled to overflowing. There the better part of two decades worth of inactivity lay in forced hibernation.

He had joked once to an infrequent visitor that they were French misfortune cookies, elegant ideas all, but absent any cookie.

The detective was tempted for the first time to abandon his ritual and to withdraw one of his wishes from the small cardboard chest and to act upon its missive as a reminder, if not a penance, then proof of his own fallibility. He could not postpone tomorrow forever.

The self promises were so readily broken, yet he permitted them to remain in his presence, each one a confession in his own scrawl. One day at a time was excellent advice in so many situations. Procrastination throughout life in furtherance of what others called a satisfying career but he recognized as nothing more solving puzzles of varying complexity and brutality.

He could collect his cases and memories, catalog them into something of popular interest,

None But the Dead, or another title similarly pithy, but he knew that thought as well would settle best among the wastes scraps of paper that crowded together before him.

After retirement he would require no past, and no realistic hope of a future. The hours would crawl by, and he would wait like a passenger at an unattended airline gate, waiting for a disinterested agent to appear from nowhere and inform him that it was time to board. In the meantime, the hours would tick, and he would sit, certain that departure would occur, exact time of pushback as vague as the destination.

Percheron had been encouraged to write a book. One person had used the word exploits to describe its suggested contents.

A book? To brag? To show people how terrible humans could be? Any history he would write would be a wrong step, for it would do nothing but raise the bar for what was unacceptable violence and cruelty.

He would sooner publish a coloring book, something sweet and innocent and imaginative for his future great nieces.

He realized the absurdity of his thought before it had completed the circuit of his brain. Peace was...something else, something other than law and order. Peace was the never encountered person of interest.

It would be terrible, the forced peace of retirement.

# CHAPTER THIRTY-SIX

Eddy had vowed to refrain from drinking, to remain sober, more or less, until the murderer was caught, or the murders stopped. He would eliminate himself as a suspect. He broke his vow before it had time to set. What if the murders stopped? How would he know? Killings were so commonplace, without rhyme or reason, let alone a detectable pattern.

He remembered having seen Percheron now and again since they both had homes in Lake Forest. That had been happenstance, like these murders. Nothing but coincidence. Weren't they?

Lake Forest. Eddy recalled the huge subdivision, a huge, planned community with neither a doctor's office, nor a shop to buy a postage stamp or a bottle of water. It was modern life, sterile and separate. He had bought a pied à terre in Norton's Commons, a well-appointed movie set, that doubled as a community. At least there one could buy a hamburger and walk home. He kept his home in Lake Forest, spending odd days and nights there.

Eddy appreciated sophisticated diversions, slights of hand fabricated to delude, delay, and delight. Men enjoyed it more than women, for men thought themselves immortal while women understood the passage of time. Immortality was much preferred, up until the end. His games were a form of murder he realized, and then banished the thought to his conscience, who might enjoy it.

Behind its back, Eddy called his conscience a motivator.

"Find a lie you can..."

"Believe?"

"That would be silly."

"What then?"

"A lie you can live with, without feeling too slimy."

Eddy lay in bed and replayed his latest conversation with Kimberly. They had gone for lunch, walking from Kimberly's house out Lake Forest parkway. In the parklike setting bordering the broad street, a man was walking his dog. The man looked away while the canine defecated, followed by the dog averting its own gaze as the human scooped the deposit into a plastic bag.

Eddy and Kimberly reached Shelbyville Road, and then crossed over to Gander's, the new East End spot, a bar/restaurant that offered the best of each, at a reasonable price. It was an American version of the Irish Rover that lay miles to the west along the same road.

Traffic was growing on the busy road; it had once been a sleepy lane but that was when Goodall's restaurant was still in business.

After they had finished their fish tacos, Kimberly said, "That was good. You only live once."

"You only live once?"

"That is more than enough if you do it well."

"And if you don't?"

"Then you don't.

Eddy, I'm religious without all the goofy parts.  God is pretty simple when you get down to it.  Look at me, I get Him.  Can we move on now?"

"Move on from God?"

"I have a life to live.  You too."

Eddy nodded slowly.

"I avoid recipes that contain equal parts hope and disappointment.  Years ago, someone advised me to ignore God, all of them. Turnabout is fair play I recall him saying emphatically.  He was one for fair play.  Stupid, don't you think?"

"Ignoring God?"

"You make me..."

"Laugh?" Eddy supplied.

"No silly."

"Oh."

"You don't make me laugh."  Seeing his reaction, she added without apology, "I make you frown.  You make me talk.  Talk is usually better than laughter.  Not always, but often enough.  Still, laughter is important."

"Oh," Eddy repeated despite himself.

"Laughter is definitely not your strong point.  Men worth keeping around have laughter down.  You can't be good at everything, she consoled.  No laughter and a big ego.  That is nitro and glycerin."

"And me?"

"I sense none of the above.  But there's hope.  I can decide later."

Eddy nodded, suddenly content to let her carry the bulk of the dialogue in what was becoming a tedious play.  She was one of the few bright spots, her voice sufficiently pleasant to overcome the doubts he had about the contents of this and other conversations. For a moment he wavered as he thought that he could easily convert this banter to a verb in one letter, and batter her to a pulp. Instead, he smiled at the woman not good enough to sacrifice to his game.

"If you find one person to love in your life you are blessed. To find one who loves you? That would be..." she had trailed off, any significance lost in the noise of a large party at a neighboring table.

Eddy had not responded, not indicated that he had not heard her.

"I'm not there with you inside your head," Kimberly stated later as they reached the back entrance to the subdivision.

"But you are, Kimberly. The good parts, the parts as they should be."

"As you want them to be."

"Your words and mine are the same. I decorate my world with your best parts."

"That is creepy. I don't like it."

"You would if you could see it."

"My better parts already do. Is that it?"

"More or less."

"Less what for instance?"

"I don't remember. Your better parts help me to forget."

"And my lesser parts can't jog your memory."

"Let's discuss something else."

But they had remained silent until they reached Kimberly's front door.

"Do you believe in soulmates?"

He laughed, then stopped when he saw that she was irked.

"No," he said, his second response affirming his first.

"I do," she said in a tone that confirmed their existence. She stared at him, awaiting a corrected answer. "Why not?" she demanded when none was forthcoming. The continued silence irked her more.

How many degrees of irk are there he wondered before he said curtly, "Soulmates presupposes souls."

"And?"

"Most of what we believe doesn't exist. I know. That is why we create them."

"Goodnight," Kimberly said as he went to kiss her. She turned and closed the door to him. Eddy wasn't sure if she heard his "Let's talk tomorrow."

Eddy stared at the ceiling. Between the two worlds of asleep and awake. Was it like the difference between alive and dead, only less so? Two realities for the living, separated and connected by a river. Alcohol helped him bridge the flow between them, although he was uncertain if the connection was a benefit or self-assigned punishment.

The victim left all behind, any and everything materially valuable. What was more valuable than his life to a victim. It was an intentional insult to the family that the extinguishing of their loved one was indeed senseless. He savored the taste of the pain he inflicted, its vibration in sympathetic with his own. He hoped that whatever deity laid claim to the

191

deceased felt as strongly the kick in the teeth as Eddy intended. He had nothing against them, but, well, everyone dies.

Each was a means to an end. Working in mysterious ways was not trademarked.

Yet he was as confused as he was before this "thing" began, his knack for vocabulary failed him. No perfect word, no arcane expression to describe this, well, thing. His inability to grasp the exact, precise term was maddening. Or simply madness, he suggested aloud.

This thing, this game he acquiesced, had no end, except for the pawns swept from the board, never to return. There was no countermove, no acknowledgement that Eddy had even played his turn. Perhaps he had not yet selected anyone affiliated with a living god. Had the superstars of the past been replaced by more tolerant, less demanding divinities, weighed down neither by dogma or the legacy sacrifices demanded by predecessors?

Eddy had heard of another murder. Who cares, at this point? Was it one of his? How many did that make? Zero? Or?

He had fantasized about killing someone. Almost anyone would do after all this time. And now that he had...he had, hadn't he, Eddy asked himself.

He felt nothing, for he recalled none of it. He felt no pleasure, no fear, just the familiar dullness of a mundane hangover.

The act had been easy. Hadn't it? Easier to kill someone...who had it been? He rolled over to glance at the patient computer screen again. The man was a stranger. What had triggered him to kill the man? Self defense? Like that other incident? He remembered that one clearly, while...

Killing a stranger had been easier, easier than killing himself. The stranger had likely been caught unawares, alive and dead in nearly the same instant.

That was how Eddy pictured it, but there was no picture, no memory, no image. Whatever had happened was as dark as the screen had become.

Killing. He had read that the best of us kill ourselves.

Eddy flipped back onto his back. Who had said that? Who had he killed?, he asked silently, his eyes staring into the rectangular darkness.

Eddy thought for the first time since he had begun this adventure that he might be caught, not by Heaven, but by earth bound police. If that happened his years of confinement would be never ending, boredom for the remainder of his life.

He nearly called it punishment. That he could take, but boredom, everlasting boredom, that would be inhuman. He would sleep. The time when his mind surrendered control and relayed existence to body. It was the hours when he did not need to be. He had snapped a photo of one of the tombstones as he had waited fruitlessly in Portland that first day.

He studied the photo, the words surprisingly legible after two centuries. Ces moments ont existe. What did they mean? Was it a simple statement, a carved plea? Was it advice? Words are what you choose them to mean. Black can be white.

"*These moments existed.*"

As his were now. But to what end, except perhaps simply an ending. Sleep, for a night, or for two centuries, that might be the best of ends.

There were so many stars in the sky, was each a foreshadow of the mass of souls he would find in the afterlife, either glowing or burning? And what of the hermits, those solitary humans who seduced their fellows by their seclusion? Where would they hide in such a crowded eternity? Or would there be nothing, nothing at all?

Eddy awakened from his dream, one he was reluctant to leave.

He wondered what it meant. Not all dreams represented something, for that would be overwhelming. The majority remain inexplicable.

But this one was different. When a dream maker takes such care, with wardrobe and setting, there must be a message in a scene so personally delivered.

It could not be meaningless. It had been precise, detailed, sequential. There had been nothing disjointed in its flow.

He had been lost in Charleston, South Carolina for some reason, possibly due to a business trip. He was on foot and entered an empty stone factory or warehouse, a building constructed to last for the century or so that it had, to fabricate an item of worth and value, an object today deserving of little more than a moment's curiosity. The walls were thick, nearly windowless, their color uniformity gray. The floor was dirt and gravel, with a few splotches of lichen or moss that survived as persistent pioneers, content to outwait the walls own obstinacy against gravity. The milieu was one of permanence.

At the end of the building, Eddy reached a large wooden staircase that veered ninety degrees to the left, and downward. The stairway was functional, while still bearing traces of elegance that workmen of the epoch carved naturally into their handiwork. It was broad enough for five people to march abreast.

The light dimmed as Eddy descended. As he reached the bottom, he found himself in a large, waiting room, furnished in rich wood, paneling behind the ornate desk, the only illumination was that provided by a squat lamp.

What fuel fired the lamp; Eddy could not determine. It could have been gas or electricity. He could distinguish very little in the pénombre, save the middle-aged woman who sat behind the desk. She was dressed in clothing appropriate to the age of the factory upstairs and the archaic office setting in which they found themselves. He was at a loss for words, given the oddness of the scene, his confusion heightened by the nonchalance exhibited by the secretary, for that was the conclusion he had reached as to her identity.

It dawned on him that he had interrupted her conversation. With her cat, he surmised at first, spotting the animal, but then corrected himself as his vision improved.

There was another woman, this one perched on an adjacent settee. She too had a cat, and they were half turned to face him.

Eddy heard or rather sensed, the presence of others in the anteroom, and as his vision reached its full capability, he counted another woman, three or four men, and another cat or so. The men and women wore business attire from another epoch, thick, warm, dark. Their attire was bearable in the subterranean coolness but would be stifling under the South Carolina sun that beat down a score of feet over their heads.

Under his own feet, Eddy noticed thick, Persian type carpet, the floor covering providing, with its few splotches of crimson and gold, the only color in sight.

The residents were nonplussed. Were they all blind, Eddy wondered.

It didn't matter. Maybe they could help. If not, he would... He would what?

Eddy took a deep breath, noticing the coolness of the underground office for the first time.

"Excuse me, I was wondering if you might tell me where I am? I was trying to..."

He did not finish his sentence immediately, as it struck him as so prosaic in such a bizarre situation.

"I am trying to get back to my hotel," he said, embarrassed."

The woman nodded soothingly, then asked, "We are about to start our bridge game. Do you play?"

Eddy woke at that moment, half wishing that he had been able to stay for at least one rubber.

# CHAPTER THIRTY-SEVEN

"Autopsies for all to watch. That might reduce crime since nothing else had. What are you guilty of?"

Percheron studied the suspect.

"Today is today," he counseled the man across time.

Was that really himself in the mirror, a man guilty of having lived too long, culpable of having grown old?

He shaved meticulously, the electric razor insistent in its buzzing, himself aware that none of the mourners would note his diligence, only its absence. He had prepared himself thusly on few previous occasions, weddings, his parents' funerals. Today's grooming would be unappreciated, as such was the nature of funerals. Percheron finished shaving and turned away from the familiar yet vaguely different face. It was time to dress and attend to a man whose time had truly exhausted itself.

Percheron had listened to numerous eulogies for business, none for pleasure. A few had been memorable, either for their excessive length, or for their embarrassing brevity. They often bookended a life, from marriage to interment, phrases intended to be meaningful, sometimes spoken by the same best man at both occasions. Invariably, they failed.

There was no explanation of the inexplicable. Words were spoken to encapsulate, or celebrate, or regret a life that was fading to memory. Words were passed to friends and strangers alike, seeded in the memory of those who would soon disperse, then not long afterwards, wither to memories of a memory. Those too would be extinguished and themselves buried.

His own job and by extension his life appeared ridiculous. He solved murders in his best attempt to prevent others, when each rescued victim was not saved, only graced with a bit more time to pass in meaningless existence. At least it got him out of the house, his own mentor had chided him all those years ago. He too was dead.

It was something for him to do, he muttered, then muttered that muttering was a sign of age. The thought annoyed him. That too was an indication of age.

Eddy's unexpected death in what appeared to be a true, simple, car accident, was a clearer finale than he had anticipated. It was time to end the case, appropriately in a cemetery, for that was where it had begun.

Words to mark every occasion, joyous or sorrowful. Today he would listen again for business and would likely utter a few of his own for the same reason. Yes, he would stand silently and listen silently.

And finally, he would speak as was not typically his wont. But today was today, maybe the last of todays, for there would afterwards remain nothing but yesterdays.

Eddy was to be interred in Cave Hill cemetery. It was the place to be remembered if not seen. A life condensed to a few words and dates; a handful of mis recalled anecdotes. Markers large and small that all demonstrated one's insignificance.

Percheron recognized a few faces. The deceased's uncle, his own niece, standing next to an attractive woman whose name he did not know, but whose face he recalled as having seen a few times at Chek's barbeque. Emerald was there, along with a few fellow detectives, mingling with the mourners. His own partner, he was there. It was good to know someone at a funeral.

Percheron observed the older man as if the for the first time. He would give the eulogy. He was the only one present who was clearly a relative. That was evident by the unmistakable facial resemblance. 'The uncle' was how the police file would refer to him for all posterity, the police file that was now nearly complete.

The man seemed distracted, but not distraught. He glanced at the sky repeatedly. Was he concerned about rain interrupting what would certainly be a brief service. Attendance was scant, more police than relatives, a few friends, one new acquaintance.

Percheron saw the man looked skyward, and the detective's followed the other's gaze. What could be so compelling in the heavens? There would be no rain today, for the sky was completely absent of clouds.

The service was indeed short. All the attendees knew their lines, their blocking. They were performers in a play that no one wanted to stage. The uncle gave a bizarre eulogy, the stranger dominated audience polite, perhaps amused. It would be recounted best over drinks, preferably outdoors. A seat near the river at Captain's Quarters would be ideal. The one under the huge oak. The mourners would need to hurry to claim it. Percheron would not be attending the after party.

"Families are strange things. You never know what you'll get."

Percheron thought of strange suspects he had encountered. Some had fled, a few had escaped, a couple had committed suicide.

"In our case it was as if we had been given a god. Gods in the family. It sounds weird, blasphemous. I'm not sure if having a god in the family is a blessing or a punishment.

He was the most successful of our clan, a god in the family is the nearest I can describe it. And now he is gone, struck down by fate. I guess that happens to all of us."

This was neither escape nor suicide, Percheron knew. A tragic accident the press had concluded, and police forensics had concurred.

"Sometime God gets it right," one of the senior lab technicians had commented.

"We fight over one god or for multiples. I see no difference."

The uncle glanced around, as perplexed at the words he had spoken, as by the fact that no one had left the ceremony yet.

"The words carved on Eddy's tombstone don't matter. He won't be returning to approve or correct them."

Percheron wondered what the words were to be, for, as of yet, the monument was absent.

"The greens keeper hears better lyrics through his ear buds. Nowadays, we have no time for the living, and the dead, well they don't respond to slights. They are allotted nothing. He is dead, forever dead. He is not coming back. And you know it. I know it. He doesn't know it, for he is gone. I miss him more than he would have noticed my absence. I suppose that grief has its own peculiar hierarchy. The most admired of us would shed few tears.

Goodbye Eddy."

The single act ran without error, yet at its conclusion, there was no applause, only the sense of a collective sigh, and a few cleared throats.

It was a gorgeous day, and the bulk of the mourners quickly left, content to have donated a few, now vanished moments of their own brief existences to Eddy's memory.

Percheron was speaking with Emerald.

"A man reads about the crime online and comes to believe that he is guilty of it. His private cosplay."

Emerald smiled at the term.

"Ash taught me that word. Sometimes they cross over. Crimes I mean."

"Boys and their silly games. And then he moves from play to reality. I heard that his laptop was filled with evidence," Emeral said as she watched the exit dwindle to a few stragglers.

Percheron raised his eyebrows at the last word.

"Men can be so fanciful," Emerald opined.

"Pride goeth before the fall," Percheron said, with a wan smile. "That is all I remember from..."

"Sunday school?" she completed.

"Detective school," he corrected.

"I don't understand how you can work in the environment you do."

She waited for a response that did not arrive.

"This Eddy must have discovered some higher power in his pride," Emerald said.

The detective remained motionless.

"It was his fantasy! Another deity to add to mankind's ever-expanding collection. He must have been insane. Murder ordained by a god to demand obedience."

"Or the reverse."

"God knows why."

"I like to think so."

"I'm sorry that we had to meet under these circumstances."

She thought this was like a blind date, everyone coy, stiff, on their best behavior. As expected, the man had chosen somewhere familiar and comfortable.

The venue was the aftermath of a murder scene. That wasn't correct, she admonished herself.

It was not his idea, she told herself. And this was not their first meeting.

Don't make a fool of yourself. Let it play out naturally. Not every scene could be orchestrated. Unless one was skilled, she rebutted herself. He would make a trophy husband.

"So am I. I regret that we crossed paths this way."

"What now?"

"Well, the case will be closed. The main suspect is dead."

"His computer was full of incriminating evidence," Ash, who stood to Percheron's right , chimed in, repeating what the woman should not have known.

"He seemed so nice. So that's it then?"

"Unless there is another crime that fits the pattern."

"There was a pattern?"

"Forget that I said that. I must be tired."

Disappointed, his colleague judged. Always the same Perch.

"Barring another crime?"

"There will be another crime."

Her surprised expression prompted him to add, "There is always another crime."

"I see."

"A new victim, a murderer, debutant or experienced. But as to this case, I'm convinced that the murders are over, the killer at peace in this cemetery."

The woman exhaled and nodded in gratitude.

"He seemed so nice," she repeated.

"He did.  And what about you?  Are you leaving Louisville in the rear-view mirror?"

"Yes, I'm afraid so."  She knew that she and Percheron would never be a couple.  "I hope that you understand."

"I do.  'Don't look back', I think is good advice.  Even a glance in the rear-view mirror will return only a distorted scene, reversed from side to side, a false trail.

If I want to contact you, where may I reach you?"

"That might be difficult as I'm moving on."

"Will I be able to contact you at the same 502 number?"

"Sorry.  I'm changing that as well."

"As well?  Is Louisville not to your liking?"

"Louisville is wonderful.  But given all that has happened.  You of all people should understand.

I can't be the first victim who has packed up and moved on."

Percheron ignored the word she used to describe herself.

"Including your cell number?  That is a bit odd."

I like to assimilate in a new town when I arrive.  A local phone number helps."

"I'm sure it does."

"You have a terrible job in a wonderful town, detective.  Its accommodating and..."

"Useful?"

"Helpful, I mean.  If you give me your card, sorry," she said sheepishly.  "I must have lost the one you gave me."

"Like your cell?"

"Yes, no. I still have the phone but with Talkatap..."

"With what?"

"A phone app. I can have a local number assigned wherever I am. It's not as odd as you might think. It prevents stalkers and, oh, other entanglements. You never know who will meet online."

"Or who has your number?"

"Yes," she began. "I hope..."

"Well, until we meet again," he said, finishing the conversation.

She nodded, went to shake his hand, and then reconsidered, as his gaze was already elsewhere.

She walked to the gravesite and paused there a moment. A lipreader would have heard, "Au revoir Cher Eddy."

Eddy dead, now buried and quickly forgotten. He had played his part well. The entire local cast had been magnificent. No, she would remember the Louisville engagement without a final glance at the detective. Her last words with the famous Percheron were pleasure enough. She had defeated the experienced detective as he was preparing for retirement. He had swallowed the red herring she had set before him. The fish himself soon to be covered with six feet of dirt before the clock of the Catholic cathedral tolled the next hour. Eddy had been such a find, a young, successful entrepreneur, that he too she had bested.

They were both insane, Eddy and she, Emerald knew. Insanity helped them both excel, although she wondered now was it too much or too little insanity that determined victory.

"He was still a boy," she had overheard someone say at the gravesite. Well, too bad, she thought. He had wanted to play with fire.

She turned and walked away. As she approached the edge of the burial party, Percheron looked at the elderly woman and nodded to his subordinate, who in turn made a hand signal to the young couple who stood astride the gravel path; Percheron's niece and her partner, two detectives.

Strange, Percheron thought, there are more relatives among the police than among the genuine mourners.

The pair of detectives separated, each stepped to one sign of the female killer and took her into custody.

When she turned to look over her shoulder to seek Percheron's attention, all she saw, as she was led away quietly, was the back of the detective as he stood over the grave of Eddy, her latest victim.

Percheron nodded again at Ash. He could take over from here. As for himself, he was tired, oh so tired. It was time to rest. There had been enough killing. God only knew.

FIN

www.ingramcontent.com/pod-product-compliance
Lightning Source LLC
Chambersburg PA
CBHW050527260626
47157CB00004B/1494